THE RANGER'S PEACE

A CLEAN ARMY RANGER ROMANCE BOOK TWO

BREE LIVINGSTON

Edited by
CHRISTINA SCHRUNK

Thank you to my readers for continuing to find my stories enjoyable.

Thanks to my critique partners, editors, and those in between for keeping me on my toes.

Thanks to my family for putting up with my long hours. I still very much want to hire a housekeeper.

CHAPTER 1

*O*f the things Ivy Manning thought she'd be doing with her life, radio talk show host wasn't one of them. It had never even been on her horizon, but an advice column gone viral four years ago had changed all that. Now, at twenty-eight, she was a household name.

The old adage *When one door closes, another opens* didn't apply to Ivy. In her case, it was all the doors flinging wide open and someone shoving her through. Fame had come calling swiftly, and her answer had been muffled by the pressure of her friend's and family's idea of success.

Do you know how many people would die to be in your shoes?

Ivy, you'd be crazy to turn this down.

Are you serious? Of course you're going to take it.

Father, mother, brother, sister, aunt, uncle, and her best friend, Missy, who was now her manager. All of them looking at her as though she'd grown a second head at the very suggestion that it wasn't what she really wanted or, at the very least, that it was happening too fast.

"Ivy? Are you with us? Or are you leaving the GripeVine hanging?"

Her producer's voice penetrated the chaos of her thoughts. Donna Jones had been with her since the beginning. A year after hosting a segment at the Gatlinburg Radio Station, Ivy had found herself with an offer at a larger station in Nashville. That was three years ago. She'd been so intimidated at first when she'd moved, but Donna made the transition easy.

Ivy smiled as she pushed all her thoughts away. "Oh, sorry. I'm with you."

"What are your parting thoughts today?" Donna asked.

Ivy pushed her chestnut hair over her shoulder. "Today, try giving back a little. It doesn't have to be a holiday or special occasion to be kind to your fellow man. Think of ways you can bring joy to the world. Give someone a compliment. Buy a stranger a cup of coffee. Open the door for that bundle-ladened individual. Brighten a person's day. Not only will you put a smile on their face, but yours as well. This is Ivy Manning. When you need to gripe, come to the vine."

Donna played the segment's end credits and music. "And you're clear."

Ivy wilted, putting her elbow on the tabletop and her head in her hand. "I'm so glad that's over. I think if I had to do one more segment, I'd scream."

"I know, and I'm sorry. We just had to get these done before you go on your book tour."

"Yeah, it's not you. It's me," Ivy said with a half-smile.

Donna roamed around the studio, getting ready for the next host who'd be on in a few minutes. "Any more from your stalker?"

Ivy nodded. "Yeah, I got one yesterday and another package a week ago. Both were a little rougher than the last few." And crazy enough, the press from the stalker had catapulted her even further.

"Still being gross?"

"Yeah, with just a few variations. I've stopped reading them. It passes through my dad to the Guardian Group. If it's safe, they send it on to me. Kolby takes care of the packages. So far, they've just been dead roses."

Donna paused her post-show ritual. "And no closer to the person doing it?"

Ivy glanced over her shoulder to Kolby, the hulking Adonis holding up the inside studio wall, throwing a thumb in his direction. "I think he answers that question."

From the very first letter, her manager and best friend since high school, Missy Lords, had taken it as a serious threat. No way was she taking a chance Ivy could get hurt.

Initially, Missy hired a local company in Nashville, but the guard assigned to Ivy failed to keep a mysterious package from showing up on Ivy's doorstep. The contents had been harmless—that time a teddy bear and a rose—but it had scared her family enough that her dad had called in a favor from a friend, and a new company was hired. The Guardian Group—a security firm of ex-Army Rangers now headed by a man named Noah Wolf. The next thing she knew, a bodyguard was taking up residence in her spare bedroom since the middle of last April. It was now March, making it a month shy of a year.

Donna glanced at the man over her glasses. "This is going to sound wrong on all sorts of levels, and I'm not discounting the threat, but, man, what I wouldn't give to be guarded by him."

Ivy chuckled. "He can hear you, ya know."

"Oh, I know. I'm single, by the way," she said and winked at him.

"You are so bad." Ivy shook her head as she stood.

She couldn't blame Donna one bit, though. From the second Kolby Rutherford showed up at her front door, she'd thought he was without a doubt *the* most attractive man she'd ever laid eyes on—tall, lithe, and muscular with a narrow waist and broad shoulders. His t-shirts fit him well, accentuating every inch of his toned chest and arms. The man was tan, like, crazy tan, with steel-gray eyes, a head of thick blond hair, a jaw that could break concrete, and his backside? The jeans he wore must have been personally made for it. She'd never been more jealous of fabric in her life.

Donna shrugged. "Can't help it." She held up a finger as if something had just come to mind. "Did I tell you Newt wanted to see you? He called me during that last segment."

Ivy leveled her gaze at Donna. "No. Why would he want to see me now?"

She shrugged. "I haven't a clue, but he sounded pretty excited, so it must be good news."

Good news to Newt meant horrible news to her. Signing on to do the segment in Gatlinburg had been fun, and watching it grow and expand to other parts of

Tennessee was neat, but getting picked up nationally had been a nightmare.

"Better go. Newt said he was grabbing an energy drink and a candy bar before he went to his office," Donna said.

Ivy groaned. "Great. He'll be speaking at the speed of light."

Donna braced her hand on the chair and laughed. "Girl, you are not kidding. Sometimes his voice is so high that I think only dogs can hear him."

Ivy grabbed her purse out of the chair by the door and stopped next to Kolby. He'd worn her favorite cologne, citrus and sandalwood. Man, he smelled good. "You may need earplugs."

He grinned. "I'll be fine."

Inwardly, she sighed. If only he wasn't her bodyguard. When she'd first met the man, he'd been rather prickly—almost harsh, *laying down the law* that he was only a bodyguard and not her friend, as he'd said some eleven months ago. He'd explained that in their line of work, it was easy to confuse professional and personal, and he didn't want any confusion. As time passed, he'd softened while still maintaining his distance and professionalism. Only recently had she even learned his age, twenty-nine. A year older than her, but the way he carried himself said his age was just a number.

Oh, but that smile. She couldn't stop fantasizing about those warm, full lips on hers. And she was doing it right that second. With him staring at her. Hot embarrassment grew in her belly and raced to her ears. No doubt he had to be wondering why she was turning sixteen shades of red.

She cleared her throat. "Okay, let's go."

He opened the door and stepped out to check the hallway before moving aside to let her pass through. At the end of the hall, Missy waited for her.

"Hey, did Newt call you?" asked Ivy.

Missy nodded. "Actually, I called him, and he gave you the message."

"You did? Why?"

Missy gave Kolby a glare. Her friend wasn't thrilled with the man. Not that she didn't love Ivy and want her protected. It just created a hassle for her with scheduling. He always had to check things out first, make sure they were clear, and do background checks on everyone in attendance.

Missy hooked her arm through Ivy's as they walked toward Newt's office. "You're going to love this."

"Well, if you're this excited, it's probably something I won't like."

"Oh, Ivy, you can't tell me you don't love this. You're known all over the country. Somewhere out there tonight is someone who followed your advice, and now their lives are better for it. You help people."

"There's also someone out there sending me threatening messages."

Ivy loved Missy and had since high school, but sometimes it felt as though she didn't hear what Ivy was saying. It was all too much. She just wanted to slow down a second. Take a breath. She went from one promotional event to the next. And the book tour that was lined up only fueled Ivy's longing to disappear for a while.

"Missy, I'm getting tired. I'd really like to take a break."

"I know, but we need to strike while the iron is hot, and right now, that iron is you. This book deal is huge. Think of all the endorsements and merchandise that could come from it. You work hard now, and you'll be set for the rest of your life."

Yep, same conversation, different verse. How about enjoying life and taking things a little slower?

"Ivy, I've worked so hard to get you these things. Staying up late hours, negotiating deals...I mean, I know you want to slow down a little, but all of it's in motion. If you back out now, it might come tumbling down. I know you don't want that."

No, Ivy didn't want all of Missy's hard work to be for nothing. The people-pleaser in her reared its ugly head, and she sighed. "No, of course not. I know how hard you've worked. I'm sure it'll be fine. On the next flight to California, I'll just put my headphones on and take a breather while I'm in the air." She smiled.

Missy patted her hand. "Exactly. We're in this together, remember?"

"I remember," she said as they stopped at Newt's wide-open office door.

He stood and grinned. "Ivy. My favorite little rock-star radio host!"

Inside, Ivy withered. He was far too happy. Bad news was a bear, and this one was a grizzly. Ivy's shoulders rounded as she sat in the chair across from his desk, pulling her purse into her lap. "Would one of you just tell me what's going on?"

Newt flicked a gaze to Kolby as he shut his office door. "I'll let Missy give the news."

"Okay, spill it," said Ivy.

Newt moved to his desk chair and sat.

Missy's lips broke into a huge smile. "You've been asked to fly to Seattle and co-host *Live with Charla*."

Ivy groaned. *"Live with Charla?"* Television? A national radio show, speaking engagements, a book tour, and now a television show? She wanted to cry just thinking about it.

"Yes. They're saying that if everything goes well, they might offer you a spot as her permanent co-host." Missy clapped her hands and squealed. "It's so great, right?

Newt grinned and nodded in agreement like a flicked bobblehead.

Ivy sucked in a large breath and let it out slowly. "I thought she had a co-host. Theresa Reid."

Missy nodded. "Well, she did. Theresa is out. Apparently, she said something on her Chatter account and created a firestorm. The network fired her. That means you've got a great shot at taking her place."

Ivy stared at Newt. "But what about my show here? Why are you so excited about me leaving? I thought you wanted me to stay."

Newt was entirely too happy for Ivy's comfort, and she braced herself for a new level of workload. "You don't have to leave. *Live* has plenty of breaks. You can do segments in between tapings and keep your job here as well as there. Missy and I have worked it out. There'll be zero conflict."

"But I've already got all of these other commitments. I've been going non-stop for more than a year now. Every time I ask for a break, I'm told just one more thing, and they turn into six, and I get no downtime." Ivy could feel the exhaustion seeping its way into her bones just thinking about the schedule they were making her for. Her throat began to close up. Gripping the edge of the desk, her stomach turned as the room spun.

Breathe. She just needed to breathe. The panic attacks were new. Another side effect of her fame. She counted to ten, then to twenty.

"Ivy, are you okay?" Missy asked. With one more deep breath, Ivy pushed the panic away. "Yeah, I'm good."

Newt had come out of his chair and now stood next to her. "I'm glad that therapist was able to help you."

"Me too," Ivy said, her voice thick. She glanced from Newt to Missy.

"I can't guys. I can't keep going. Don't you understand? I need a break. All this going and doing and never a minute to myself is too much. Please give me a break." She didn't care if it sounded like she was begging.

Missy cupped Ivy's shoulder with her hand. "It's

just one shoot with *Live*, then I promise I'll schedule in a break."

Tears threatened. "When do they want me?"

Missy grimaced. "The network wants you there in two days. You'll leave at four that morning so you can be at the studio by six for hair and makeup. They want to do a run-through before they shoot live, too." She paused just enough to catch her breath. "They've even booked you the presidential suite at the Four Seasons."

"Absolutely not," Kolby said in his slow Southern country-boy drawl. Oh, man, Ivy dug his accent, even though at times, she had no idea what he'd said, and she'd have to ask him to repeat himself. "We had an agreement. You make the schedule far out enough that I can thoroughly clear people."

Missy lifted an eyebrow, a smirk on her lips. "I'm sorry. I couldn't understand that. Could you speak a little slower?"

Ivy could take a lot, but she hated it when Missy was snobby to Kolby, the one side of her friend she'd never understood. Missy could be so sweet and kind, helping Ivy at the shelters, walking dogs, all the community service things that Ivy loved. But it seemed impossible for her to be nice to Kolby. "Missy, don't be hateful. He's doing his job."

"Why did your dad have to hire him? Surely there

was someone else...more refined." Her best friend crossed her arms over her chest. "Someone who could speak a language we understand."

Ivy twisted in her seat to look at Kolby. "I'm sorry."

Missy glowered at Kolby. "The network is sending a private plane. They know about the stalker. Their guys would have cleared everyone anyway."

Kolby's jaw clenched, and he kept his expression neutral. "But they aren't me. I'll need to speak with the security team and have my people do background checks on them as well."

"Don't you think that's overkill?" asked Newt.

Kolby shook his head. "No. Her safety is my job, and I do my job well. Get me the name of the company. I'll make sure they're vetted before she gets on that plane." His gaze lowered to Ivy's. "That's if Miss Ivy wants to go."

Ivy smiled at Kolby in appreciation. *Miss Ivy.* The way he said it sent a shiver through her. That was as close to calling her by name as he'd get. She was his client; therefore, she deserved respect. Turning to Missy and Newt, she said. "I'll do the show, but I'm done for a while after that."

Newt and Missy began to speak at the same time.

"Guys, I'm going home for now," Ivy said, standing.

She leaned into Kolby. "Like I said, I'll do the show, but after…I don't know."

Kolby hooked his arm around her shoulder, and she let him lead her out of the room. It had only been recently that he'd been doing little things like this. Part of the reason she'd begun to fantasize about kissing him. She felt safe with Kolby. Of course, his salary put a damper on things.

If only she had someone who loved her and put her first without getting paid to do it. Maybe when she finished shooting *Live with Charla*, she'd take a break and reevaluate where she wanted to go in life. She was tired of being alone. This time next year, she wanted to have someone's arms around her who she loved and who loved her.

CHAPTER 2

A hearty beef smell floated in from the space between the bottom of the door and the floor of the bedroom Kolby Rutherford had been calling home for almost a year. Closing his eyes, he breathed in the aroma. Holy smokes, his client could cook like nobody's business. Based on the delicious scent, it was beef stew. And man, he loved that stuff.

When he'd first met Ivy, he'd made sure she understood he was her bodyguard and nothing else. They weren't friends and were never going to be. His experience with rich people was limited to his stepdad and those in his circle. All of them were snooty, condescending, and came across just as cruel as the man who'd married his mother.

Not beautiful Ivy Manning, though. She was nothing like what he'd expected. Kind, giving, personable, and sweet, with infectious laughter and a face definitely made for something more than radio. Geez, she was pretty. Long, wavy chestnut hair that she'd pull into a messy bun, but somehow, it would look perfect. Dark eyes, a button nose, long legs, and the perfect height to kiss her forehead without bending over. That was saying something, too, because he was over six feet tall. She also had the most perfect set of lips God ever painted on a woman. And this one lone freckle peeked from her hairline that seemed to beg to be kissed.

It was if she'd been handcrafted for him because Ivy had everything he'd ever pictured wanting in a woman.

The world was cruel, though, and she was off-limits. It didn't stop him from praying that maybe God would have mercy on him and let him have a chance to see if things could go anywhere with her...after he was finished guarding her, of course.

A rapping came at the door, and he yawned. He'd escorted Ivy home from the radio station, made sure the house was safe, and retired to his room to do his typical checks for when they were going anywhere in public. Missy had to stop springing these trips on him. It took time to make sure people checked out.

Nearly a year had passed since the Guardian Group was hired by Ivy's father, James Manning, and they were still trying to catch a break. Ryder, his buddy and the best computer guy in the world, couldn't get a lead on who was sending the nasty emails. Even Mia, Noah's new wife, was helping him, and from what Ryder said, Mia was as good or better than him…and he'd sworn Kolby to secrecy on that.

He stretched his arms over his head, stood, and walked to the door. He opened it and nearly sighed. She was in jeans, a simple t-shirt, and no makeup. His favorite look for her.

Ivy smiled. "Dinner's ready. Are you hungry?" He liked that little Tennessee accent too. It wasn't as thick as his, but it was just enough twang to render him speechless at times.

His stomach grumbled. "Uh…" She often cooked for him, but he'd typically take his meals to his room. It helped him keep some separation. Something he needed, especially when she looked so cute.

"Sounds like you are," she said with a laugh and pointed to his stomach.

"Yeah, I'm hungry. Thank you." He followed her to the kitchen where a bowl was already waiting for him.

It made him wonder what she'd planned if he'd said no.

Picking it up, he took a deep breath and said, "I don't know what you put in this, but I've never tasted anything so good as your beef stew."

A gasp brought his gaze to Ivy. Her lips were parted like she was shocked. "You've never said you liked it. I thought you did, which is why I cook it more often now, but…" She grinned. "I'm glad you like it."

He rubbed the back of his neck. "Aw, you don't have to cook it for me. I appreciate it, though."

She pointed to the chair across from her. "Sit and eat with me?"

"Uh, well—" Eat with her? Lord have mercy. He couldn't.

"I get that you've got to keep things professional, but you can do that and have a conversation. I'm sure your bodyguard training included eating meals with clients."

He chuckled. No, there was nothing like that, and even if there was, it wouldn't have prepared him for a meal with Ivy. She was alluring on every level. "I'm not sure there was course in that, but—"

"Kolby, please? I'm begging you. Just sit down and eat with me."

Aw, she was breaking out the *please?*

She jutted out her bottom lip and batted her lashes. She'd never done that before. What new level of temptation was this? Talk about unfair. How was he supposed to resist that? Would it hurt to sit at the table and eat a meal with her? He was a professional, right?

"Okay, Miss Ivy, I'll eat with you," he said as he set the bowl down. He walked to her chair and held it for her.

Again, her lips parted in surprise. "I don't think I've ever had a man hold my chair for me before. Thank you." Her smile widened as she took her seat. It was dazzling. Like he'd given her an award or something rather than just doing a simple thing like being a gentleman.

Then what she'd said hit him. "No one's held your chair?"

"No, but it's not like I date a lot."

"That's not a bad thing. It's better to have one good date out of two than six out of a hundred."

She laughed. "Well, when you put it like that."

"Oh, I didn't mean—" His cheeks burned as he rubbed the back of his neck. He didn't need to be eating with Ivy. She was so out of his league, she was in a different galaxy.

"I know what you meant. I was teasing you."

"Oh. Right." He needed to be quick and get back to

his room. Bowing his head, he folded his hands in his lap and said a silent prayer of grace. He always prayed for their safety as well. That God would give him the smarts to protect Ivy.

When he lifted his head, she was staring at him. "Do you pray every time you eat?"

"I try. Sometimes I can be forgetful, but I think He knows that and forgives me."

"I don't know why, but I didn't picture you as a Christian."

He shrugged and scooped up a spoonful of stew, blowing on it. "Aw, that's okay. I'm supposed to be invisible so I'm not in your way."

Her lips twitched up, and she held his gaze. "I don't think you can be invisible, Mr. Rutherford."

"Heh, yeah. I do try, though."

"I know, and I appreciate it." Her gaze lowered to the table. "You're no closer to finding out who the stalker is, are you?"

Kolby shook his head. "No, but we won't stop until we do. I'm sorry you're stuck with me."

She lifted her gaze to his. Is that what smoldering looked like? Because if it was, and she did that a few more times, he'd be doomed. "Oh, I can think of worse people to be stuck with."

Oh, mercy. He was a frog in a pot almost ready to

boil. Warning bells were going off, but if he bolted, it would hurt her feelings. How on earth was he going to get out of this? "I should probably take this to my room and continue my security checks."

"Please don't go. This is fun. I like talking to you." She smiled.

She liked talking to him? "I think that's the first time anyone's said that to me. Most of the time—" He stopped short. She didn't need to know personal details about him. That was a surefire way of getting into an even bigger mess of trouble. That's why he used her name so much. Miss Ivy. It was to remind him she was his client and he needed to be professional.

"Most of the time what?" She tilted her head.

He waved her off as he stood. "Aw, nothing."

Ivy jumped to her feet and walked to him. "No, don't go. We're just talking. I want—"

A knock came at the door, and Kolby said a silent thank you. "Were you expecting anyone tonight?"

Shaking her head, she said, "No."

"Any packages?" She was supposed to let him know when she was expecting packages so he wasn't surprised when they showed up.

She chewed her lip and nodded. "Yes, and I forgot to tell you. I ordered a birthday gift for my nephew. I wanted to wrap it first, so I had it delivered here. I'm sorry."

"It's okay. Just let me check it first."

She blew out a frustrated puff of air and said, "I hate this. I hate this fame. I hate all of it."

Pushing her hair over her shoulder, he slid his hand from her shoulder to her wrist and said, "We'll find out who's threatening you, and then life can go back to normal. I promise."

He knew the instant she took his hand in hers that he'd made a mistake. Zaps of electricity arced across his skin and made his nerves tingle.

"That means you'd be leaving, right?" she asked.

"Yes, ma'am."

She held his gaze a moment, and then a smile spread on her lips. "Not sure I like that."

There was enough tension in the air that Kolby could bench press it. He swallowed hard and stepped back. "Let me get that package."

"Okay."

Forcing himself to pull his gaze from hers, he walked to the door and checked through the peep-hole. He drew his gun, opened the door, and checked the surrounding area before holstering it and picking up the box. The second his fingers touched the package, he felt weird. He dropped it and slammed the door before setting the alarm system.

"Is something wrong?"

"Call 9-1-1," he said. "There was something on the package. Tell them…" He leaned his back against the wall and slid down as the room spun. "Tell them not to touch it."

Kneeling next to him, Ivy held the phone to her ear. "Yes, this is Ivy Manning."

While she called emergency, he quickly sent a text to Noah, his friend and boss. He stuck his phone back in his pocket and tried to listen as she told them what was happening, but he'd barely managed to send the note to Noah, and his ability to focus was fading.

"She's asking me how you're feeling."

"Heart's racing, dizzy, really tired all of a sudden, a little sick to my stomach."

Ivy reached for his hand, and he jerked it away.

"No, it's a contact poison. Don't touch me."

Ivy relayed his symptoms to the operator. "An ambulance is on the way, as well as police."

"When they get here…" He took a deep breath and tried to remember what he needed to tell her. "You stay at the house, alarm on, and—" The sentence died on his lips as he slid sideways to the floor.

His last thought was that Ivy's stalker had turned

dangerous. No longer just sending packages that were filled with cute things or emails. Whoever it was had advanced to trying to kill her now. Hopefully, Kolby would stay alive long enough to see the creep brought to justice.

CHAPTER 3

he sound of the hospital door opening
pulled Ivy's attention away from Kolby.

Missy's head popped in, and she frowned. "What
are you doing here? Weren't you supposed to stay
home with the alarm system on? The police would
have stayed with you."

"Shhhh…" Ivy put her finger to her lips and stood.
She brushed the back of her hand across Kolby's
cheek. He'd protected her at the risk of his own life.
She'd thought she understood what that meant. Seeing
it firsthand, it made it real.

She walked to the door and slipped out, facing
Missy. "I'm fine. I'm in a hospital. If something's going
to happen to me, wouldn't this be the best place?"

Missy hugged Ivy. "I'm just glad you're safe. Why didn't you call me right away?"

"Because there was nothing you could do."

"Do they know what it was yet?"

"Nicotine poisoning. They said if it had been a little stronger, he wouldn't be alive. I had no idea there was even such a thing."

It had been so frightening. Kolby went from being healthy and fine to on the floor, passed out in minutes. He could have died because of her, and after their little not-quite-dinner and his comment about leaving, the thought of him not being around tugged at her heart.

Missy blinked. "Nicotine poisoning? I've never heard of that either. But then again, I don't go around stalking people and trying to kill them."

"If I'd touched that package, it would have been enough to kill me. I'd fallen into the trap that the stalker was harmless and gross, but this was scary. I don't know about doing the show in Seattle. I think Kolby is right. We need to wait so he can do the proper checks on people."

"The studio isn't going to let anything happen to you. I've even lined up a new bodyguard to go with us."

Tilting her head, Ivy furrowed her eyebrows. "A new bodyguard? No. Kolby is my bodyguard."

Her friend narrowed her eyes. "You've got a thing for him."

A thing? No, she didn't have a *thing* for him. She had a ginormous crush on him that had sort of turned into a little more as she sat with him in the hospital. He was cute as could be, and now he'd saved her life? He'd gone beyond cute to knee-knocking, sweating palms, hot-as-a-tin-roof. But telling Missy that? No way. Ivy would never hear the end of it.

"I don't have a 'thing' for him. If I'd told him about the package, maybe none of this would have happened. He risked his life for me, and I feel responsible because I didn't follow his instructions. That's why I think we should wait to go to Seattle."

"Fine, but if he's not ready to go by the day after tomorrow, we're leaving without him. The studio isn't going to wait for him to get well, and we've made a commitment."

Ivy nodded. "All right, but they said he only needed to stay overnight for observation. He'll be able to travel by then."

"Now that you know he's okay, do you want me to give you a lift home?"

"No, I brought clothes so I can stay with him. I'm not leaving him alone in this hospital."

Missy crossed her arms over her chest. "Ivy, you need to go home. It's safer there."

That wasn't happening. She looked over her shoulder at the door. The thought that Kolby could wake up alone bothered her. "I'm staying. I'll be fine. As soon as the doctor releases him, I'll go home."

"Okay, then I'm staying too. Just let me go home and get some clothes."

Ivy shook her head. "No, you work enough as it is. Go home and enjoy your evening."

For a moment, Ivy thought Missy would argue, but, shockingly enough, she nodded, gave Ivy another hug, and left as Ivy went back into Kolby's room.

Ivy crossed the room and sat beside him, taking his hand in hers. If nothing else, she wanted to be next to him when he awoke so she could apologize for being so careless.

Maybe twenty minutes later, he slowly opened his eyes and blinked. "Miss Ivy?"

"I know you said to stay at the house, but I couldn't let you come here alone."

Lifting his head, he looked around. "How long have I been here?"

She smiled. "Just a few hours."

He glanced down and tried to pull his hand from

hers, but she tightened her grip. "Do they know what it was yet?"

"It was nicotine poisoning, and you're fine now. They're keeping you for observation."

"You shouldn't have come. What if—"

Ivy leaned over and kissed his cheek. "You saved my life. I'll never be able to thank you enough. It's my fault you're here. If I'd done as you asked, told you about the package, it wouldn't have happened."

"Aw, no. There's no telling what happened. It wasn't your fault. It was the stalker's."

"But I should have listened. I dismissed the threat as being benign, and it wasn't. You were so sick, and I was worried. I promise I'll be more careful from now on."

He covered her hand with his free hand. "It's okay. You've never experienced this before, and until now, there's been no reason to think you'd be attacked. I should have been more careful. It's my own fault."

She circled her arms around his neck. He was being so sweet, taking the blame when it wasn't his to shoulder. She'd never met a more selfless man. "I'm so glad you're okay."

For a brief second, he froze before wrapping his arms around her.

Minute after minute ticked by as he held her, and her heart seemed to race faster and faster as he did. He pulled back, cupped her cheek, and smiled. "I'm glad you're okay. I dropped the ball. If something had happened to you, I'd have never forgiven myself."

It was a good thing she was at the hospital. If her heart raced any faster, she'd need resuscitation... preferably by the gorgeous man taking her breath away.

Her gaze dipped to his lips and back up. God have mercy, and it was a genuine cry for help. If she didn't back away, her heat-seeking lips were going to lock onto his against her permission. That wasn't totally true. More like against her better judgment.

A knock came at the door, and Ivy bolted to her feet. She was hot from top to bottom. There were probably volcanoes cooler than her.

"Come in," Kolby said.

Ivy tucked a piece of hair behind her ear as a man entered, followed by two other large men. "Oh, hi, Mr. Wolf." She'd met him a month after her dad first hired the Guardian Group when he took over the company.

"Miss Manning," he said and smiled. "This is Elijah and Mason."

"Hi."

"If you don't mind, I need to talk to Kolby."

A moment of panic sliced through her. Was Kolby going to get fired? "It wasn't his fault. I'm the one who didn't tell him about the package coming. If anything, blame me, not him."

Noah chuckled. "No one's being blamed."

"So you aren't firing him?"

Mason snorted. "Sorry, that's funny."

"Oh, well," Ivy said and caught Kolby's gaze. There was a look in his eyes she couldn't put a finger on, but if she were a guesser, it was him thinking she'd lost her marbles. It was the night of embarrassments and a good time to get out of the room and regroup. "I'll go get something to drink so you can talk."

"Let Elijah escort you. Just to err on the side of caution," Noah said.

"Sure."

What had come over her? She'd nearly hyperventilated at the thought that Kolby wouldn't be around anymore. Good grief. Kolby had only recently started actually speaking to her.

Except he had saved her life. That was probably it. Yeah, she was crushing on him, but she wouldn't be crushed if she had to be guarded by someone else. Her heart whispered, *Not true.* Not like she could argue, either, unless she just wanted to lie to herself.

STERILE, WHITE, AND COLD. OKAY, NOT WHITE, BUT soothing beige. As if a color could make him feel better about being in the hospital. After spending as much time in one as Kolby had, it wasn't soothing. It only grated on him.

"Hey, Noah. You sure you don't want to fire me? I shouldn't have picked up that package," Kolby said as he sat up. "What I did was dumb."

Noah and Mason stopped by his bed and each shook his hand.

He loved both of them, but his relationship with Noah was different. They'd both been tortured longer than the other guys. Both had nearly died. Noah was a good guy, and Kolby couldn't imagine working for a better man.

When Kolby first started working for the Guardian Group—well, not just him; it had been Noah, Ryder, Gunner, Elijah, and Mason—they'd been working for a woman named Pamela Williams. She'd started the security firm when her husband was murdered, and he'd left her a sizable fortune. Right before Kolby began working for Ivy, she'd stepped down, and now his buddy Noah was calling the shots. Not much had changed since he'd taken over, except the person signing his checks.

"I've done worse," Noah said.

Mason nodded. "Yeah, he has."

As a field medic, Mason Andrews had more than earned Kolby's respect, even if he didn't know much about the man. Mason was a good guy, but he was tight-lipped about his family. It made Kolby wonder if they had more in common than he thought.

Noah rolled his eyes. "Shut up."

"I'm going to get a copy of the blood sample results before we leave. See if there's anything I can find," Mason said.

Noah crossed his arms over his chest. "And Ryder and Mia are going to dig a little harder too. Now that the stalker has made a move, you're going to have to be extra cautious."

Kolby rubbed his face with his hands. "I know. Did Ryder get the background checks done for the trip to Seattle? That is, if she still wants me to go."

Mason snorted again. "With the way that woman was looking at you, we were lucky we got her out of the room. She likes you."

"Stop that. She's too…everything for the likes of me. Listen to me. I sound like an idiot," Kolby said, the tips of his ears burning. Ivy didn't think of him that way. She was just being nice. Sure, she'd flirted a little, but that didn't mean anything. Like she said, she hadn't dated a lot recently, so she was just lonely and he was available.

Mason shrugged. "I'm calling it like I see it. The look on her face when she thought Noah was going to fire you? Man, it was fierce. You weren't leaving without a fight."

"Why are the two of you here other than a blood sample?" asked Kolby.

Noah dropped his arms to his side. "We wanted to make sure you were okay, and we're going to check around the house. Make sure the police didn't miss anything."

Mason nodded. "Liquid nicotine poisoning isn't something that just happens. Someone had access to it, the ability to cover the box in it, and we're betting this was a good thing. I think it might be the break we've been looking for."

Kolby shrugged. "I think they can send me home, honestly. It's stupid to stay in this hospital when there's nothin' wrong with me."

The door to his room opened a fraction. "Is it safe to come back in?" Ivy asked.

"Yep, all done here," Noah said.

Ivy pushed through with Elijah following. "Kolby, I

brought you something to eat in case you were hungry."

Mason caught Kolby's gaze and then flicked his eyes to Ivy. "See?"

"Shut up and go away." Kolby flopped back on the bed.

Mason turned to Ivy. "He's going to try to convince you he doesn't need to be observed, but don't listen to him. Staying will be good for him."

Kolby bolted upright. "Don't listen to him. He's messing with me. I don't need to stay overnight. I'm fine."

Ivy covered her mouth as she chuckled.

"Okay, we'll get out of the way," Noah said. "Miss Manning, if you need anything, don't hesitate to call, but you're in good hands."

She smiled. "Thank you. I think so too." She caught Kolby's gaze and held it.

"And that's definitely our cue to leave," Elijah said. "We'll see you later, Kol."

"Yeah, see you later."

Once the guys were gone, Kolby rubbed the back of his neck. "I'm really okay to go. If you'll step out, I'll get my clothes on, and I can get you home."

"No, the doctor said you needed to stay overnight just to make sure." She walked to him and handed him the bag she held. "That's a sandwich and a water. I've noticed you don't like ham, so I got turkey on wheat. No tomatoes or lettuce. Just mayo, mustard, meat, and cheese."

He hadn't expected her to be that observant. "Uh, thank you."

"And I got UNO and a deck of playing cards to keep us occupied if there's nothing on TV."

"Aw, you didn't have to go to all that trouble. And you don't have to stay either. Really, I'm fine if you want to go home. I'll get Noah and the guys back in here to make sure you get safely home."

She sat facing him. "I'm good. Eat so we can play cards. I'm in the mood to kick someone's behind at UNO."

"Is that right?"

"Yep." Her eyes twinkled.

"You think you can whip me?" He shouldn't be flirting back, but it was too hard to refrain when she was being so cute.

Ivy nodded. "Oh yeah. I am an UNO queen, buddy. I'll have you in the fetal position in two hands."

Kolby snorted as he pulled his sandwich out. "Then I'm not sure I want to play someone as tough as you."

"Hurry it up, mister. I've got itchy hands."

Oh, she was something else. He couldn't resist the

pull she had on him. It was wrong, and he couldn't let things go any further than a little flirting and a card game. Flirting was harmless, and playing cards was okay. He could manage those and keep his heart in check.

CHAPTER 4

By the time Ivy and Kolby were dropped off at her home, Kolby was itching to be back on the job. He hated that he'd been forced to stay at the hospital all night and that it was after one in the afternoon before they'd finally managed to discharge him. And for what? Nothing was wrong with him, and he knew it.

After checking the house and the area around it, he stepped back inside and set the alarm system. "Everything checks out. I'll be in my room if you need anything."

"Nope."

He tilted his head. "Nope?"

"You owe me dinner. You said you'd eat with me,

and we didn't get a chance to do that. I'm going to make dinner, and you're going to help me." She smiled.

"Aw, I—"

She narrowed her eyes. "Are you one of those men who think women are the only ones who should be in a kitchen?"

He blinked. What on earth? "No, of course not."

"Then make yourself useful. I was thinking we'd have chicken fried steak and mashed potatoes."

His stomach gurgled. It sure did sound good. Aside from the beef stew she made, that meal was in a tie for his favorite. "All right. If you think I can be useful, I'll help."

She smiled. "That's the spirit. Now, you can peel the potatoes."

He nodded, found a peeler, and quickly got to work, liking the rhythm of doing something that felt productive. Mostly he'd stayed in his room while he lived there because he didn't want to be in the way, and because it was easier to remain detached. Once people started sharing meals and all that, feelings could bubble up, and he didn't need help in that area. Ivy was something special, and to him, she was pretty near as perfect as a woman could get on earth.

"How long have you worked for the Guardian Group?" asked Ivy.

"Oh, a few years now."

"Do you like it?"

He shrugged. "I enjoy the work. It makes me feel useful and gives me something to do, and I get to help people."

Ivy filled a skillet with oil and set it on the stove to heat. Then she set up dishes with flour and milk to dredge the steak in. "Have you been a bodyguard for a lot of people?"

"Not a lot, but enough to keep me busy."

"What type of people have you guarded?"

Kolby chuckled. "All sorts, really. From businessmen to kids who were caught in custody battles."

She turned to him, a smile on her lips. "Have you fallen for any of the people you've guarded?"

His hand slipped, and he sliced his finger. Putting it to his lips, he dropped the peeler and rushed to the sink to rinse it off. The question threw him. No, he'd not even been tempted until Ivy. Did she know that? If he'd been as smooth the last few months as he was just now, she probably did.

"Uh," he said as he ran the water over his finger. "No, I've never fallen for anyone." And even if he had, it took two. With the way he talked? No one would want him.

"Let me see it." She took his finger in her hand. "It's

not too bad, but it's the little ones that sting the worst. Let me get you a bandage."

Before Kolby could object, she walked to a drawer at the far end of the kitchen and pulled a box out, returning with it.

"Do you have to work to keep yourself unattached to people? I think that would be the hardest part. Not getting emotionally attached. I don't think I could do it," she said as she dried his finger off and wrapped the bandage around it.

His hair had to be standing on end, the way her electric touch was messing with him. "It's not easy sometimes, but…"

Her gaze lifted to his, and he was momentarily speechless. God had crafted her from only the best materials, because she had to be, hands down, the most beautiful woman he'd ever seen. And with her looking up at him, her eyes sparkling, it was enough to give him a heart attack.

"But what?"

"I talk funny, and it makes me sound like I'm dumb. Nobody's gonna want me, so I keep that in mind." He swallowed hard. He hadn't meant to say that, but it had poured out. It would only make her feel sorry for him, and he didn't want that.

She shook her head, her eyebrows knitting

together. "That's not true. You don't sound dumb at all."

His chest tightened as he thought back to his step-dad, the things he'd say. People were going to be nice, but anyone in their right mind wouldn't give Kolby the time of day. Not really. They were only being polite, saving face, so to speak.

"Aw, Miss Ivy, thank you for being nice." Heart hurting from the memories, his stomach churned. "I'm not hungry anymore. If it's okay with you, I'll just go to my room."

Kolby didn't wait for an answer, he just left. It might have hurt her feelings, and while that wasn't what he was trying to do, he had to go. He had an image to maintain, and looking like a wimp wouldn't help. Personally, he didn't think showing emotion made him look weak, but that didn't change reality. Men couldn't cry or be upset. That wasn't macho or heroic.

He stepped inside the room she'd given him. It was a good-sized area. A queen bed, a dresser, and a small desk filled the space without making it look over-crowded.

Folding into the chair in front of the desk, he pulled his computer closer and checked his email to see if Ryder had finished his check so Kolby could have some peace about going to Seattle. Missy seemed to think that just because some big studio said things were okay that they were, but he'd been around long enough to know that just because you were fancy didn't mean you were right.

He leaned back in the chair and crossed his arms over his chest as he let his eyes glaze over. Why had he said all that stuff to Ivy? What had possessed him to even mention it? He'd never done that before. For the life of him, he couldn't understand what it was about her that made his tongue so loose.

His phone rang, and he checked the caller I.D. "Hey, Noah."

"Hey. Everything okay?"

No, but what did it matter? A crummy childhood didn't have any business interfering with the present. And it wasn't like anyone could change anything anyway, so what was the point in saying something? "Yeah, it's good. Is something wrong?"

"We believe the poison came from an area in North Carolina. It's consistent with the type of tobacco grown in this area."

North Carolina? That's where Guardian Group's home base was, but there was something niggling in the back of his mind about it. Something that rang familiar, but Kolby couldn't put his finger on what.

Then again, he'd gone over so many details in the last few months that it wasn't surprising that facts blended together. "Okay."

"We're still looking into who could have obtained it, but for now, at least, we have an area to start with."

"We're leaving for Seattle in the morning. I've sent you a schedule, the group the studio hired, and the private jet company we'll be using. Was Ryder able to check it out?"

"Yeah, everyone's clean."

Kolby was hoping that would give him some peace, but it didn't. He'd had a growing nag in the back of his mind that something didn't sit right about the trip, but a feeling wouldn't keep them from going. "I'm gonna make a couple of survival packs."

"Why? They're clear."

"I don't know. I've just got a feeling, and I can't shake it. Better to be prepared, right?"

"Just a feeling?"

Kolby smiled. "All right, I feel like God's telling me to make them."

"I'll never understand you or that whole 'God talks to me' thing, but whatever works for you."

"You don't have to." Kolby chuckled.

Noah paused a moment. "You sure you feel okay? I can send Elijah if you don't."

"I'm fine. I was fine last night, but that doctor made me stay. Well, him and Ivy."

"I think Mason's right. I think she likes you."

"Aw, Noah, don't you start. I'm not good enough for the likes of her."

"I didn't think I was good enough for Mia—still don't—but I get to go home to her every night, and I'm forever grateful I was wrong."

Kolby picked at the edge of the desk. "It's different with Ivy and me, and you know it."

"Don't let your prejudices against yourself bleed onto her. She seems like a woman with a keen mind and the ability to make decisions on her own."

Noah didn't understand. Kolby loved him, but coming from money and a good family, Noah would never get that Kolby just wasn't on the same level as him or any of the other guys. And no matter how much his friends tried to say otherwise, once it was beaten into a person that they were trash, it was hard to change that mindset.

Kolby sighed. "I like her, but she should be with someone that won't get her made fun of. She needs someone that can smile for a camera and stuff like that."

"Or maybe she needs someone who will love her

when the cameras are gone and there's no one left but her and the person she loves."

"Aw, Noah, can we drop this? I need to pack for this trip."

"Sure, but I'm right."

Kolby rolled his eyes. "You think you're right all the time."

Noah laughed. "Because I am."

"Let me go. I'll talk to you later," Kolby said, ending the call.

Whatever Noah thought could happen, wouldn't. Ivy Manning was poised and refined. She was a Southern Belle, and that kind of woman didn't fall for the Kolbys of the world. At least, not this Kolby. It wouldn't take a second for Ivy to figure out she'd want someone better. Why would he subject himself to that sort of heartache? Nah, better to pine from a distance than get hit with a tree.

A KNOCK CAME AT IVY'S BEDROOM DOOR. PUSHING HER covers off, she stood and walked to the door, opening it. Kolby filled her doorframe. Somehow, he always managed to look good and smell even better.

With the way he'd run from the kitchen earlier, she hadn't expected to see him until morning.

He thought he sounded dumb because he talked with such a thick accent, but she didn't think that. And the haunted look in his eyes...she wasn't sure she'd ever forget it. Then he'd hightailed it to his room.

After, she'd put the food away, nuked herself a bowl of soup, packed for the trip in the morning, and settled into bed with a book. She'd thought about him the whole time, wondering if there was anything she could do to help make him feel better. He didn't sound funny, and she didn't think he was stupid.

"Hi. Are you okay?" she asked.

He nodded. "Yes, ma'am. I'm sorry for leaving so abruptly earlier, but...anyway, I was wondering if you're going to pack any warm clothes."

She tilted her head. "Why?"

"Well, I've learned it never hurts to be prepared, and it can be chilly in Seattle. If you'd be so kind as to pack a few warm things, I'd appreciate it."

Part of her wanted to press him because it felt like there was a bigger reason, but instead, she said, "Sure." She chewed her bottom lip. "Kolby?"

Lifting his gaze to hers, he said, "Yeah?"

Oh, those gray eyes of his. They made her knees weak every time. "I'm not sure what happened earlier, but I don't think you talk funny or sound dumb. And that's not because you saved my life. I really do love your accent."

His lips curved up. "Aw, it's okay."

She stepped into him, placing the flat of her hand against his chest. "No, really. Kolby, don't listen to people like Missy. They're wrong. You have a beautiful accent and a voice I could listen to all day. I like your laughter, what little I've heard, and you're brave and heroic. You served this country, and if anyone doesn't see that and appreciate you, it's their loss, not yours."

Heartbeat after heartbeat pounded before he nodded. "Uh, thank you for that, but you don't have to be nice to me. I'll protect you no matter what you think of me."

What could have happened to him to make him think so poorly of himself? "Then it's a good thing I think so highly of you. I may not know you as well as I'd like, but from what little I do know, you're a good man, Kolby Rutherford. And no accent's going to change that." She lifted on her toes a fraction and kissed his cheek. "I'll always be grateful you were assigned to protect me. I think I got the better end of the deal."

Holding her gaze, his fingertips grazed the spot

she'd kissed. "I should go. Don't forget to pack a few warm things, okay?"

She smiled. "I'll do that right now."

He tapped the doorframe with his hand. "Good. I'll see you in the morning," he said before taking a few long strides and disappearing behind his bedroom door.

Ivy shut her door and leaned her back against it. That man made her a gooey mess. His voice, the way he smelled, his smile. There was nothing about him that didn't check her boxes. She straightened, walked to her closet, and began pulling out warm clothes to pack.

Her stalker needed to be caught so that Kolby wasn't her bodyguard anymore. Normally, she'd want the guy to ask her out, and she still did, but if he didn't, the second Kolby Rutherford wasn't her bodyguard, she was taking things into her own hands. If he was half as great as she thought he was, then he was a man worth breaking convention for.

CHAPTER 5

*P*itch black. The new moon coupled with the cloud cover threw an ominous feeling over everything as Kolby rode in a limo with Ivy and Missy to the airport. Whatever it was about this trip that felt off to him was only growing the closer to the airport they got. He just wished he could put a finger on why.

Ryder was the most thorough guy Kolby knew when it came to background checks, and everyone had come back clean. At least, that's what Noah had said and what Ryder's email confirmed. Well, minus the one schmuck who couldn't stop parking in front of fire hydrants and had racked up a boatload of tickets.

And yet, Kolby's gut gnawed at him, and the little voice in the back of his head said, *Be alert and ready.*

Which was why he'd brought two packs of survival gear. He hoped she'd listened and brought some warm clothes.

"I know you said it's better to be prepared, but that's a lot of gear," Ivy said.

This morning, she'd quickly showered, raked a comb through her hair, and thrown on a t-shirt and jeans. The scent of whatever shampoo she'd used filled the limo, and it took work for him not to close his eyes and inhale.

He lifted his gaze to hers. Scaring her for no good reason didn't seem like the right thing to do, especially when he didn't have anything but a feeling and the idea that he'd been told to do it. "Nah, just prepared."

"Is that from your time in the Army?"

He shrugged. "Yes, ma'am."

"I told you. You don't have to call me ma'am or Miss Ivy. Plain Ivy is just fine." Her voice was so sweet, but that was because Kolby thought she was sweet. Not that he should think that way, but he was a man, and she was special, and he slipped sometimes.

"I'm sorry. I can't do that."

Missy grumbled under her breath. "I don't understand why you keep this guy. Just ask your dad for a different bodyguard."

Now, that woman? Oh, she was attractive, but,

man, they were oil and water from the moment he'd taken the job. He couldn't understand what Ivy saw in her. Missy never listened to Ivy, always pushing her to go. With friends like her, who needed enemies?

Ivy switched seats in the limo, taking a spot next to him and laying her head against his bicep.

Kolby froze. Things had been changing between them for a while, but stuff like this still caught him off guard at times. He couldn't say he didn't like it, though. He liked Ivy...more than he probably should.

Ivy glared at Missy. "I like Kolby. I feel safe when he's around, and I like his accent. If you can't stop being mean to him, I'll go to Seattle without you."

Her saying that in front of Missy made him think that maybe she wasn't just being nice the night before.

She'd defended him before too, though a little more subtly. He both loved it and hated it when she did that. Loved it because she was standing up for him, something he wasn't used to, and hated it because it made keeping his professional distance all that much harder.

The night before when she'd kissed his cheek, it had taken a strength he didn't know he possessed not to take her into his arms and give her a good and proper kiss. It would've been a dumb thing to do, though. He was convinced she was just being nice, and that didn't give him justification for planting one on her.

"I'm not being mean. He's an employee. Yes, he saved your life the night before last, but you'd be just as safe with someone else," Missy huffed.

Ivy hugged his arm, and tingles raced in every direction. Normally, he'd feel uncomfortable with someone doing that, but she was different. He didn't mind her doing it.

"Missy, I love you, but you need to stop," she said. "Just because he's an employee doesn't mean you can treat him just any old way you want. Now, apologize for being hateful, and don't do it again. Understand?"

Kolby turned his head away so they couldn't see him smile. If only Ivy would stand up for herself like she stood up for him, then she might not even be on the way to the airport. Why couldn't her friend see how tired and sad she was? If the hateful woman really cared about Ivy, she'd stop scheduling every second of her day and let her get some rest.

"Fine. I apologize, Kolby."

And skunks don't stink. Some apology. Sarcasm laced each word.

Ivy tightened her grip on his arm as if to say she was sorry for the way her friend was behaving. "That wasn't a real apology. You're better than that."

"And you're better than him," Missy grumbled.

He wasn't sure if Ivy heard it or not, but he had.

The limo came to a stop, and Ivy released her hold on Kolby. As he opened the door, Ivy glared at Missy and said, "You're dead wrong about that."

He climbed out of the vehicle, checked the surrounding area, and motioned for her to exit the car.

As she stepped out, she paused in front of him, her eyebrows drawn together, and cupped his cheek. "Don't listen to her, okay?"

The tingles elicited from Ivy hugging his bicep were minuscule compared to this touch. Zaps spread from her hand, warming his skin all the way to his bones. Lost in the moment, he covered her hand with his. He'd have been worried about all the little touches that morning if it weren't for the fact that she was just trying to be nice. "You're a special lady. You know that?"

Tears reflected in her eyes in the dim light of the airport. "That means something coming from you."

"Are you going to keep me waiting in this limo all day?" Missy asked.

A pin touching a balloon wouldn't have popped as quickly as the moment they'd shared.

Kolby cleared his throat and dropped his hand. "I

need to get you out of the open and onto the plane. You're a sitting target out here."

Nodding, Ivy stepped away from the door, and Missy followed right behind.

"Geez, Ivy, what were you doing?" asked Missy.

"I was thanking Kolby for protecting me."

Missy rolled her eyes. "Yeah, because he's not paid to do it."

Ivy's lips trembled. He could tell she was tired, which meant she must have been restless the night before. No doubt worried about the show she'd be taping today in Seattle.

She lowered her gaze and said, "Yeah, because no one could care about me if they weren't paid." Her voice was so soft that Kolby almost missed it.

Now he hated that he was getting paid. "Are you tired?"

Her gaze lifted to his, and he could see it in her eyes. "Exhausted."

"Want me to carry you?" The words had tumbled out of his lips without a second's consideration. He was there to protect her, right? Didn't that mean mentally too?

Slowly, the corners of her lips lifted. "Would you really do that?"

"If you want me to, I will."

Missy snorted. "Oh, good grief, Ivy, what is up with you this morning?"

Turning an icy glare toward Missy, Kolby swept Ivy into his arms. "I'm taking her to the plane," he said, taking long strides away from Ivy's friend, not stopping until he'd set Ivy down in one of the seats. He took a knee in front of her. "Are you sure you want to go to Seattle?"

She nodded. "Yeah, she's worked really hard to get me this far, and I don't want to let her down." Even tired, she was beautiful. She had such a giving heart, and to Kolby, that made her ten times more attractive than the average pretty girl.

"Okay, I'll get the luggage on the plane." He smiled.

Ivy caught his hand in both of hers. "Would you stay with me? The crew can get the luggage."

Kolby hesitated. He usually loaded their stuff. "Won't Missy need to sit with you?"

"She can sit somewhere else this morning. I just...I know you're getting paid to protect me, but it would be nice to lean against you. You don't seem to want anything from me, and I appreciate that." She sighed and cast tear-filled eyes to the floor. "That didn't come out right. I know Missy loves me, but—"

"You need a break?"

Lifting her gaze to his, she nodded. "Yes."

He'd protected a good number of people, and never once had he felt such an overwhelming desire to hold and care for someone. The luggage would find its way on the plane without him this morning. "I'll sit with you," he said, settling into the aisle seat next to her. "Miss Ivy?"

She set her head against his bicep. "Yes?"

"Would it make you feel better if I didn't get paid? I mean, I've saved most of what I've earned because it's just me. I do this kind of work because I like to feel useful. To make a difference in the world. If it would—"

Ivy leaned back, her eyes locking with his and her lips parted. "You'd really do that?"

He nodded. "I'm here to protect all parts of your life. If it would help you, make you feel safer or better, I would."

Her words seemed stuck on her tongue as she opened and shut her mouth a few times. "No, I don't want that, but I can't say it isn't flattering to know you would." She stretched her arm across his chest and rested her head in the crook of his arm. "I just need some sleep, and I'll stop being so whiney. I get like this every time I don't sleep well. You'd think I'd learn by now."

The thought occurred to him that ditching her the

night before might have been the cause, but she didn't think of him like that. She was doing a live television show, so she was probably worried about it. "It's okay, Miss Ivy. We all have our moments." He slipped his arm around her shoulders and hugged her to him. "You get some rest. I'll wake you when we get close to Seattle."

The fabric of his t-shirt moved as she moved her head up and down. "Thank you."

Just then, Missy stepped through the cabin door, shooting daggers in his direction. She rolled her eyes as she strolled to a stop in front of them. "How cute. You can move now. I need to go over a few things with her."

This woman had hit his last nerve with a hammer. "She's tired. Whatever you need to go over can be done later."

"Ivy," Missy snapped.

Ivy lifted her head a fraction, her eyes barely open. "I can't, Missy."

"But—"

Kolby held up a hand. "She said no." He pulled Ivy onto his lap and wrapped his arms around her.

Ivy's body melted against his as she took a deep breath, and he knew immediately that he'd made a mistake by holding her. He needed to keep their relationship professional, but he'd said he'd protect all of her, and that's what she needed at the moment. Someone to hold her and stand between her and the world. "She needs some rest."

Missy worked her jaw, mumbled something under her breath, and stomped to an empty seat two rows ahead.

Man, he couldn't stand that woman. Ivy deserved better than the likes of that viper. Sliding his hand down the length of her hair, he touched his cheek to the top of her head. From this point forward, he was going to stand up for her. If she needed to feel like someone cared about her, then he'd take that on as one of his duties. Ivy was his client, and he'd do that for anyone he protected.

The little voice mocking him in the back of his mind could stuff it.

CHAPTER 6

*A*fter dropping their luggage off at the hotel, Ivy and her crew had been chauffeured to the studio. It had taken hours to do hair and makeup, wardrobe, and the run-through. Ivy didn't like any of it, least of all Charla.

Currently, they were live, with screaming fans plastered against the window behind them. Charla leaned across her chair, placing a hand on Ivy's fore-arm. "Ivy, I have to say it's been a real pleasure having you co-host today. You are just a breath of fresh Tennessee air."

Ivy couldn't roll her eyes; it'd be rude, especially on national television. It sure didn't stop her from wanting to. There was no way she could stick with this gig on a permanent basis. Not with Charla Far as the co-host.

If the woman were any more fake, she'd be a statue in a wax museum. It was two seconds after they'd hooked Ivy up with a mic that Charla had floated in, gracing Ivy with her presence. It had been awkward and weird and uncomfortable. Charla had hiked her leg and marked her territory. A territory Ivy wanted nothing to do with, but she'd promised Missy she'd keep that nugget to herself.

The only comfort was knowing Kolby was standing off to the side, just out of sight in case anything went wrong. She didn't know what it was, but it felt as if something had changed between them. It had felt good to sit next to him and wrap her arms around his bicep. There were so many zaps that she'd expected to pull back a blackened hand. And then he'd carried her to the plane.

Not that he was anything but professional, but the butterflies in her stomach danced the cha-cha. It did make her want more, but she also knew Kolby's desire to maintain his professionalism, even if the distance between them seemed to shrink the longer he protected her.

He'd offered to guard her for no pay. That had touched her heart so deeply. Even though he'd been grumpy when he first started, she'd sensed he had a gentle soul, but that offer had confirmed it.

Then he'd pulled her across his lap, wrapped those incredible arms around her, and held tight. She knew he was just fulfilling his promise to take care of all of her, but that move had been the absolute cherry on top of her crush sundae.

Now, she was flat-out smitten with the man. Beyond smitten. Her crush was cruising down a highway that, if she were honest, was both exciting and scary. What if he didn't think of her that way? She *was* his client, and he *was* a professional.

"Well, thank you," Ivy replied to Charla. "This was fun. I appreciate the invitation." And she'd be telling Missy that under no uncertain terms was she ever hosting this show again. The people-pleaser in Ivy had her limits, and Charla had beaten that limit to death with a sledgehammer.

Charla turned her cheesy smile to the camera and said, "That's all for us today. Tomorrow, we'll have Paul Grainger, author of the hit series *Portal Escape*, hosting, along with some cooking tips from Chef Weinhard, owner of Bistro Viva, and musical guest Marla Knowles."

As the cameras stopped, a curtain fell over the window, and Charla's smile was gone in an instant.

"Listen, if you get this gig, you need to understand not to step on my lines. There's a reason the show moved from New York to Seattle. I'm the star, and don't you forget it."

Ivy smiled sweetly. "The only way I'd host this show is if it was a cold day in—"

"Ivy, that was awesome," Missy said, pulling her into a bear hug. "Just awesome." She turned to Charla, and they shook hands. "Thanks so much for extending so much hospitality. This has been an incredible experience. Really, really incredible."

Charla greedily ate the compliments. "Oh, of course," she said and eyed Ivy.

Geez, the woman was two-faced. How could Missy not see it? Or could she, and she didn't care?

"Yeah, it was great." Ivy pulled her mic off and handed it to the sound guy. There was a technical name, but she'd forgotten it. To her, there was no point in remembering since she'd never have use for it again.

Charla smiled. "Well, I need to go. Enjoy your stay in Seattle." The woman sauntered off.

Ivy turned to Missy. "This isn't for me."

Missy sighed. "Look, we've got a lunch meeting with two of the network execs. Let's see what they have to say. You can always say no. Plus, we have that very cushy hotel suite to take advantage of."

"What's the point in having lunch? I'm saying no. I don't care what anyone has to say. I don't want to do this show."

"It was scheduled before we arrived. They wanted to take you to lunch to say thank you and to discuss things."

Ivy knitted her eyebrows together. "I thought you said you'd give me a break after this."

Missy squared her shoulders and crossed her arms over her chest. "I am. Why do you think I negotiated that suite? But the taping came with a meeting. It was a package deal. Did you really think they wouldn't want to at least speak to you after?"

She pinched her lips together. What was going on with Missy? They'd been friends forever, but lately it seemed as though Missy only saw Ivy as a commodity. "This happens every time. You say I only have one thing and then I can take a break. When I do that one thing, you slap on another. I'm sick of it. Why can't you understand that I'm tired? I need a break. One night isn't enough."

Kolby's presence behind her didn't need an announcement. Not only could she feel him, but his rich cologne tickled her nose. "Are you okay, Miss Ivy?"

Missy's lips spread into a thin line. "Look, Superman, Ivy's fine. Just stand over there and leave her alone."

Ivy turned to Kolby. "I'm okay. We're having lunch with two of the network executives." Hiding her frustration with the situation was beyond her means.

He cut his gaze to Missy and back to Ivy, obviously clued in that she was upset. "Do you want to do that?"

"I don't mind. It's just talking, and I *am* hungry." She smiled. "Are you hungry? I noticed you didn't eat this morning."

"I'm fine, Miss Ivy."

Rolling her eyes, Missy shook her head. "Could I please talk to you in private for just one second?"

Ivy took his hand and squeezed it. "Just give us a minute, okay?"

He nodded toward the backstage exit. "I'll be over there if you need me." She shouldn't have watched him go, but that backside of his was a hard thing to ignore.

"Okay, Missy, what?" Ivy asked.

"Listen, he's cute. I'll give you that. But your career is just taking off. You don't need to be in a relationship right now. Not only that, but your world is about to open up to a whole new level of men. Sophisticated, educated, wealthy men. Men with influence and aspi-rations. Don't settle for some backwoods hick who can't speak clearly enough to be understood most of the time."

Ivy gritted her teeth. "I'm not starting a relation-ship, and if I was, I wouldn't be settling. Why can't you stop being so caught up in the glitter and see the gold right in front of us? I don't need endorsements, book deals, or merchandise to be happy. I was happy in Gatlinburg with my little radio show. And Kolby Rutherford wouldn't be settling. He's the kind of man you hope to meet. Protective, kind, and gentle." She glanced at Kolby. "I like him."

"You don't even know him. Not really."

"He's been staying at my home since he started protecting me. I know we haven't delved deep into each other, but I've spoken to him a little. Why are you trying to push me away from him?" she asked, trying to understand why her friend was so dead set against Kolby.

Missy grunted. "I've poured my heart and soul into this. Right now, a relationship with anyone isn't good timing. I'm looking out for you. Those charities you like donating to? How would you give them so much money if you weren't where you are? That's because of me and my work. We're best friends. I love you, Ivy, and I wouldn't work so hard if I didn't."

"I know you do, and I appreciate everything you've done for me. But—"

"Then act like it. Lately, all you've done is gripe and complain. I'm not the enemy."

Ivy pinched the bridge of her nose. "I'm not saying you're the enemy, Missy. I'm just exhausted. I need that downtime we talked about. A vacation with peace and quiet and no schedule."

"And you'll have it. Right after this luncheon. I mean, it's lunch, Ivy. Not scaling a mountain."

Dropping her hand, Ivy relented. "All right, but just lunch. After this meeting, I'm taking a vacation. Do you understand?"

"Totally." Missy smiled.

"Let me tell Kolby so he can do his job. I know you get tired of it, but he's not the enemy either. If you're going to take out your frustrations, take it out on the person who created this situation. Not Kolby."

Missy let out a breath. "You're right. I'm sorry. But you can't get involved with him, Ivy. This job of his isn't permanent. When the stalker is caught, he'll leave to protect someone else. He'll carry *them* to planes and all the things he does for you. He's paid to do it."

The monumental effort it took to not tell Missy

that he'd offered to forgo pay was almost more than Ivy could handle. "I know. I'm not getting involved with him. He's my bodyguard." At this point, Ivy was willing to say anything to Missy to get her off this "no relationship" junk.

"Good. I don't want you to get hurt." Missy touched her arm.

Ivy nodded and left Missy to speak to Kolby. He slipped his phone in his pocket as she stopped in front of him. "Everything okay?"

His gaze caught hers, and she got the strangest feeling from him. An invisible line was always present between them, but it had been thinner lately, especially after he'd held her on the plane. Now, it felt like it was a foot thick. "Everything's fine. You havin' lunch with those people?"

"Yeah, Missy worked hard to set this up. It's just lunch, and then I'm taking a vacation." The next thing that fell out of her mouth wasn't planned. "Since you'll be guarding me, anywhere you'd like to go? Maybe we can both have a moment's peace." She smiled.

Those steely grays held hers briefly before he shook his head. "Nah, you pick wherever you want. You'll be protected no matter what." The rigid stance of his body screamed something wasn't right.

Why did it sound like it wouldn't be him? "Please

don't let Missy get to you. I know she can be a real pill, but I like you guarding me. Truth be told, Kolby, sometimes it feels like you're the only person who cares." She worked to keep her emotions in check. "You'll guard me, right? You won't leave me, will you?"

He softened ever so slightly, holding her gaze just a touch longer than normal. "You have me until you no longer want me."

What would he say if she answered with forever? "Thank you."

Kolby pushed her hair over her shoulder. It was moments like these that made her wonder if there could be something more for them. His paycheck didn't account for the tender way he touched her or the sparkle in his eyes when he looked at her. "You say the word, and I'll take you away from all of this to where no one can find you until you want to be found."

It sounded heavenly, especially if that somewhere included a beach, her in his arms, and him kissing her. "I may take you up on that offer." She chuckled and then did something she shouldn't have done. She hugged him around the waist. "Thank you for being so kind to me."

The hard muscle in his back flexed under her flattened hands as he froze. Just as she began to think it was a mistake, he wrapped his arms around her, and she wanted to melt right then and there. So much warmth and comfort from such a small gesture. "Miss Ivy, it's going to be okay."

"Are you her bodyguard or her boyfriend?" Missy barked, killing the moment.

Kolby jerked away. "She's right. I apologize, Miss Ivy."

Ivy wanted to devolve into tears. He was holding her, and she was enjoying it. Why did Missy have to ruin it? She glared at Missy. "He was just being nice."

"He's here to do a job, and hugging you isn't it."

Working her jaw, Ivy fought back her anger. "Look—"

Missy held her hands up. "I'm sorry. You're right. A new leaf is hard, okay?"

Ivy studied her a moment. She had no idea what was going on with Missy, but Ivy was growing tired of her attitude. Perhaps it was time to think about cutting ties. She'd always love Missy as a friend, but her role as manager seemed to be overshadowing their friendship the longer it went on. "When we get back to Nashville, you and I need to have a talk. A serious one about our future. You understand?"

Missy flinched back. "What?"

"We'll discuss it later."

"Okay," she said, holding Ivy's gaze a moment. "I came over here to tell you they're waiting for us."

The more Ivy thought about it, the more confident she became. Her partnership with Missy was over. She loved her, but their current situation wasn't working anymore.

CHAPTER 7

The fancy restaurant the television people took Ivy to was something else. Kolby's time as a bodyguard had afforded him the opportunity to grace the inside of many nice restaurants, but none of them compared to the insane opulence of this place. He was surprised they weren't sporting solid-gold forks.

He trailed behind the group, sweeping his gaze around the room and listening to them chatter as the hostess seated them at a table. Ivy and Missy sat together while two network executives, Lynn and Eve, sat across from them. They held such a greedy glint in their eyes, disturbing Kolby immensely. They didn't see Ivy as a person. She was a thing to be used to make them money. All he could do was pray that Ivy would stand her ground and tell them no.

Ivy stood and pulled another chair to the table. "Here, Kolby, you can sit."

His whole world was in turmoil. He'd soured when he'd overheard her telling Missy he was just her bodyguard, and the reaction had shocked him. It shouldn't have, but over the last few months he'd made the mistake of blurring the lines, and all of the touching lately just made them fuzzier. Instinctively, he'd called Noah to ask him to give him a new assignment. Noah had argued that he needed to stay. That his feelings would only fuel his determination to protect her. In the end, Kolby had won. They'd decided there would be a change in guard when he and Ivy returned to Nashville.

It had lasted all of five seconds. Ivy turned those teary doe eyes on him and pleaded with him to stay, and he'd caved quicker than a mountain filled with dynamite. Then like a fool, he'd let Missy catch him hugging her, but his way out was gone. He'd promised to stay with her, and he couldn't break it. Once they'd reached the car, he'd sent a quick text to Noah, letting him know Kolby was staying put. The response garnered a silent cuss and a quick prayer for better control next time for both his tongue and his dealings with Ivy.

"I'm okay," Kolby said.

She smiled. "I know for a fact you're starving. There's no way a man your size can't be." She leaned in, her sweet cherry-vanilla scent heightening his awareness of her. "Sit by me, please."

"I—" Whatever food this place was serving had him on a lure. His stomach growled loudly.

Ivy giggled. "I'm the boss, right?"

"Yes, Miss Ivy." He smiled.

Those thick butterfly lashes of hers batted, and her dark-brown eyes danced with mischief. "The boss is telling you to sit and having something to eat."

Right then, he'd have probably barked like a dog is she'd asked him to. Yep, square in the middle of that gold-fork restaurant. "Okay."

He held her chair and then sat next to her, his hands folded in his lap. His job was to stay out of the way, but she was making it difficult to do that when she was using her feminine wiles on him. He couldn't exactly blend in when he was parked right next to her.

"Does the bodyguard really have to be at this table? There are plenty of empty tables around. We'd like this meeting to be private," said Eve, the executive sitting across from Ivy.

Under the table, Ivy covered his hand with hers,

squeezing it in a silent cry for support. She needed him to stay where he was, and he would. "He really does, and he's a professional. What's discussed at this table will never leave his lips. Isn't that right, Kolby?"

"It'll never leave my lips," he said softly. They didn't care. They just didn't want him at the table. Of the things he was an expert on, not being wanted was one of them.

Lynn, the executive sitting across from Missy, snorted. "That's some accent."

Ivy squeezed his hand again. "It's a beautiful accent." Her gaze met his. "I like it." She was the only person to ever say anything like that, and now she'd defended him not only in front of Missy but two snooty television executives.

Most people made fun of him, which is why he didn't socialize much. The little church he'd been attending in North Carolina was small and mostly elderly. Those little old ladies seemed to like him, but he suspected they'd like anyone who mowed their lawn without being asked. He sure hoped Elijah was keeping his word to keep their lawns up.

A waiter stopped at the table, dropping off glasses of water. "Drinks?"

Kolby stuck with water while the rest of the group ordered. Ivy opted for sweet tea.

Once the waiter was gone, Missy leaned forward with her arms on the table. "So, what did you want to discuss?"

The executives exchanged looks, and Eve smiled. "Ratings aren't in, but, Ivy, you tested well this morning. You had great chemistry with Charla."

Missy inched further to the edge of her seat.

From what Kolby observed, Ivy couldn't stand Charla, and the feeling was mutual. Where the executives got that great chemistry was a mystery to him. He sent up a little prayer that Ivy would get the boost she needed to stand up to these people.

Ivy nodded. "Oh, good." It was obvious from her tone that this wasn't going the direction she wanted it to go.

Lynn nodded. "But you weren't really testing as a co-host. You were testing to replace Charla."

"What?" asked Ivy. The words came out rushed, and Kolby couldn't say he wasn't shocked too. From what he'd learned overnight, Charla was a big deal. Ivy getting the spot as the host would mean big things for her.

Eve leaned in. "Charla's contract renewal is coming up. Her numbers aren't what they used to be. Word of her obnoxious behavior has gotten out, and our viewers aren't tuning in anymore."

"She's lost most of the younger demographic, and our advertisers are bailing," Lynn said.

Ivy shrugged. "Okay."

The talking paused as the waiter returned with their drinks and took their orders.

Once he was out of earshot, Eve said, "You're young, fresh, and new. You've got a pretty face, and you come across as friendly and approachable. You'd be just the shot in the arm to give the show a boost. We'd even be willing to let you test a host and pick them, as long as they fit well."

Missy splayed her hands on the table. "Are you offering Ivy the chance to host her own show? Really?"

"Yes. You'd co-host over the next few months, and we'll not be renewing Charla's contract. You'll be the new *Live with Ivy*," Lynn said.

"That's incredible." Missy beamed.

"No," Ivy said. "I can't."

Missy cleared her throat. "Well, before we give our answer, why don't we eat and discuss some of the specifics? I mean, we *are* hungry, right?"

Ivy looked at Kolby. "Yeah, we're hungry." He could sense she wanted to go, but she was staying for him because she knew he was hungry. Which he was, but if she wanted to go, he could do without.

"I'm okay," he said. "We don't have to stay."

Her lips twitched up. "Not according to that growling stomach."

He rubbed the back of his neck. "Uh, I'd be fine."

Missy, Eve, and Lynn continued to discuss Ivy until their meals arrived and carried on through lunch. The more they talked, the closer Ivy moved to him and the less she ate. Their discussion was upsetting her, and they were so caught up in it that they didn't bother to see the effect it was having on her.

Near the end of the meal, Lynn cut a glance in Kolby's direction. "Of course, once you start working here in Seattle, the show will take care of your protection."

Ivy's head snapped up. "What?"

Kolby didn't miss Lynn catching Missy's gaze. He suddenly got the distinct impression that Missy had spoken to these women a little more than she'd let on.

"We just think that for appearance's sake, it'd be best if we took care of security," Lynn said.

"Kolby's not going anywhere, and I'm sure Missy's told you that I'm really not interested in taking the job. Things in my life are hectic enough. I barely get to see my family in Gatlinburg. I can't handle any more."

Missy patted her hand. "Give it time to settle. She'll come around."

Now it was Kolby's turn to lend her some strength.

He took her hand in his, squeezing it, and threw a glance upward as a reminder to God of his prayer that she'd be able to stand up for herself.

Ivy shook her head. "I'm not coming around, Missy. I'm tired. I've told you that repeatedly. I've also told you I like Kolby. He's my bodyguard, and he's staying."

Bodyguard. It wasn't a dirty word until recently, but he couldn't think like that. Ivy was having a hard enough time without him adding to it.

"Ivy, the book tour is only a few months, and it's concentrated on the West Coast. You could do the show, fly to the signings, and then fly back. It would be a piece of cake." Missy twisted a bit to look at Ivy.

"You had this planned," Ivy whispered. Her breath became labored. The onset of a panic attack. She gripped the table, closed her eyes, and counted. It took her until thirty to gain control. When she could speak again, she said, "You booked this, and when I asked you for a break, you lied to me." Ivy came out of her chair so quickly that it fell back. "I'm not doing this show. I'm sorry my manager wasted your time, but as you can see, we're having a difference of opinion regarding my schedule."

As Kolby stood, he picked her chair up.

"Ivy, sit down. You're causing a scene and embarrassing yourself." Missy's gaze darted around the restaurant. "And me."

Ivy straightened her shoulders. "I don't care. I'm taking a break. I'm going to walk around Seattle, head back to the hotel to get some rest, and then I'm taking a plane back to Nashville tomorrow where I will be planning an even longer vacation." She grabbed Kolby's hand, spun on her heels, and pulled him out of the restaurant.

She marched more than a mile before slowing. Whirling around, her face was stained with tears. "I'm so sick of people not hearing me. Why can't they hear me, Kolby? Am I so invisible that no one can see me?" She buried her face in his chest and sobbed.

"Miss Ivy, I think you need some rest. I think you're exhausted and burned out. How about I take you to the hotel so you can relax?"

Through a fringe of tear-coated lashes, she looked up at him. "You're getting sick of me, aren't you? That's why you were on that call this morning? You didn't want to be my bodyguard anymore because I'm an emotional wreck?"

Kolby shook his head. "No, that's not true." A half-lie was still a lie, but he didn't have the guts to tell her he'd tried to get a new assignment. Not when she was hurting like she was.

She palmed her forehead. "I have a headache, and I've never been this out of sorts in my life. I feel so out of control."

This woman needed to get her footing. She was tired of people treating her as though she didn't have a voice. He'd been guilty of the same when he told her she needed to rest, only he felt his intentions were a little purer. Still, she needed to feel like she had choices.

"Miss Ivy, what would you like to do? We will go and do whatever your heart desires, and if anyone tries to stop you, they'll have to go through me." He smiled.

Her gaze lifted to his again. "Would you go shopping with me? I promise I won't drag you to a million places."

"I will do anything you want."

"I want to shop 'til I drop." She laughed.

He laughed with her. "And I will carry you home if that happens."

She took in a lungful of air. "Thank you for listening."

"You're welcome."

Holding his gaze, she touched his face, lifted a little, and kissed his cheek. "I don't care what those jerks say. I love your accent."

Her soft lips had touched his skin again, and now he was in the middle of a five-alarm fire. "But you can't always understand me!"

"At first I couldn't, but I listened a little harder, and now I'm a Kolby-language pro." She grinned.

He shouldn't be returning her smile. That was flirting with her. But Lord help him, he couldn't stop himself. "You don't say."

She captured that luscious bottom lip in her teeth. "You know, you're really cute."

The kiss on the cheek had set him on fire, and now she was throwing gasoline on it. He needed to get himself out of this conversation before he found himself knee-deep in a heap of trouble. "Miss Ivy, where would you like to start shopping?"

With a smile, she wrapped her delicate slender fingers around his wrist, twirled in place, and trotted on. They walked miles, wandering through every inch of Pike's Market and through the downtown area.

As far as shopping went, it wasn't the worst trip he'd experienced. The highlight was how alive Ivy looked. The world had slid off her shoulders, and she was free to be happy. She laughed a little more, smiled wider, and her eyes found a little more of their sparkle.

The last stop of the afternoon was a little coffee

shop where she ordered them each something to drink and a piece of pie—without asking him what he'd like.

"Eat up," Ivy said.

Kolby smiled. "What if I don't like pecan pie?"

She leveled her eyes at him. "Kolby, you're as country as the sun is yellow. You can't tell me you don't love pecan pie."

"Just 'cause I'm country don't mean I have to like it." He chuckled.

Slicing a fork through hers, she asked, "You don't like it?" She popped a generous bite into her mouth.

"Nah, I like it. It's sweet, though, and I can't ever finish a piece."

Ivy sighed. "Good, because that would be like saying you don't like hot boiled peanuts. You do like boiled peanuts, right?"

"I could eat a bushel o' those."

"Me too. But all we'll get is roasted out here in Seattle. I did a little search on my phone last night. You can't even get boiled peanuts at a baseball game. It's like heathens are running the place."

Kolby snorted as he tipped his head back and laughed. "I'd say so if they've turned their noses up at a good boiled peanut."

Ivy grinned. "You know you've got a pretty fantastic smile, right?"

"Aw, nah, I'm…"

"Blushing like a June bride?"

He shook his head. "Now, Miss Ivy…"

"And the blush just gets darker."

"Stop that now." He sobered. "Miss Ivy, I don't want to hurt you—"

Ivy held up her hand. "Wait. Don't. I know. You're my bodyguard, and you can't get involved with me. I'm just teasing. I promise." Her shoulders rounded. "I do wish you'd stop calling me Miss Ivy. It makes me feel old and feeble. I'm twenty-eight. Just call me Ivy."

She was only a year younger than him. Well, less than that. He'd celebrated his birthday just a few weeks ago, only she didn't know that. "All right…Ivy."

"Now, did that hurt?"

"Like a rusty needle in the eye."

Shaking her head, she muttered something. The only thing he caught out of it was "men." She pointed her fork at him. "I'll figure you out, Mr. Rutherford. Just you wait."

Smiling, he dipped his gaze to the table. He wished he hadn't promised her he'd stay. The only thing the day had taught him was that Ivy Manning was bright, funny, and vivacious, even more so that he'd previously thought. She had a wicked sense of humor and a sweet smile. It wouldn't be hard to fall for her.

He could almost hear his heart breaking as she hummed while eating her pie.

CHAPTER 8

Using the keycard, Kolby entered the suite first as Ivy waited. He stepped to the side and let her in, allowing the door to swing shut behind them. She followed him as he walked down the hall to the sitting area where Missy was waiting.

With her arms folded over her chest, she seethed. "Where have you been, Ivy? I've been calling all this time."

Kolby dropped Ivy's shopping bags by the wall. "I have to clear the rooms."

"Okay," Ivy replied.

Missy glowered at Kolby as he left them to talk. "You embarrassed me today. I set this whole thing up for you, and you stormed off? Do you know what it took to keep them from completely writing you off? The excuses I had to give?"

Ivy titled her head. What would it take for her to understand Ivy was done? "Good. Let them write me off. I told you I'm done."

"You've said that before, and you've come around. What's gotten into you, Ivy? I've killed myself to get you these opportunities, and you just throw them away? Doesn't my hard work mean anything to you?"

Ivy walked to the couch and leaned her hip against the back. "You're right. I have given in before, but I'm not anymore. I know you've worked hard, but it hasn't been for me. I've asked you to stop piling things on me, but you keep going and then emotionally manipulate me until I cave. Well, I'm not caving this time. Missy, I'm an emotional wreck. I feel like I'm in chaos right now. I need you to be my best friend and not my manager for a moment."

"I am your best friend. This is a fantastic opportunity. Do you know how many people would love to be in your shoes?"

"Great, give them my pair."

Missy clenched her jaw. "I don't understand you. You've got the world in your hand, and you're just letting it slip away."

"No, I don't. I have a stalker, a schedule I can barely handle, and I've started having panic attacks. I'm not asking for anything other than a break. And I need more than a few hours on a plane from one event to the next."

"I know the stalker isn't great, but they haven't tried anything. And honestly, it did give you a boost in the public eye. And the panic attacks are under control. I saw one start today, and you handled it quickly. You'll get a break. I promise."

"Haven't tried anything?" Her voice rose. "They almost killed Kolby and would've killed me if I'd touched the package. When, Missy? When will I get a break? Give me a time frame. From what date to what date? Because you keep saying I'll get a break, and it never comes."

Missy dropped her arms and cast her gaze to the floor. "I don't know. You've got the book tour, new segments to tape, and the publisher is asking for another book."

"Another book? When were you going to tell me?"

"After we got back to Nashville."

Ivy straightened. "After I'd agreed to do the show?"

"Yes." Her tone was clipped, as if she was the one being led on a leash instead of Ivy.

"You need to stay somewhere else tonight. We need a break. I love you, and I'm angry. I don't want to say anything I'll regret. I'll book you a different suite, but you can't stay here. I need some space."

Shaking her head, Missy pinched her lips together. "You are so ungrateful."

"I am not ungrateful. I'm exhausted. I've been saying it. You just haven't been listening."

Missy snatched her luggage sitting against the wall and pulled it behind her. "Don't worry about getting me a room. I'll take care of myself. You sure aren't."

When had her best friend become so manipulative? Had she been like this the whole time and Ivy was too blind to see it? Or had she been giving excuses for Missy's behavior? Either way, Ivy was wising up, and it wasn't happening anymore.

Kolby had taken his typical position by the door, hands clasped in front of him and a stoic expression.

Missy paused in front of him, pointing her face up at him. "You'll never be good enough for her. Whether she's a household name or not. You know it, I know it, and deep down, she knows it."

It was quick, but Kolby cut a glance at Ivy. She could tell by the look in his eyes that the sound bite had dug its way into his heart. It wasn't true, none of it was, but once something like that was said, it was hard to dig it back out.

"Don't listen to her," Ivy said.

"You should," Missy replied as she opened the door. "She'll cause you to fall in love with her and then step on your heart. Oh, she'll pretend she doesn't mean to, but she will." With that, Missy strolled out, her venom lingering in the suite.

Ivy wilted against the back of the couch, her face in her hands, tears spilling down her cheeks. She'd had fights with Missy in the past, but this one was by far the worst. Her friend had come out throwing knives, and they'd all hit strategic places. Ivy was bleeding to death from the cut of her words.

Strong arms embraced her, gently holding her against a solid wall of muscled chest. "It's okay, Ivy. You needed to do that. It'd been a long time coming. If she's really your friend, she'll see this as a wake-up call. That she needs to make amends and apologize."

"Kolby, tell me you aren't going to listen to those hateful words. I don't believe any such thing. You have to know that I would never hurt you on purpose."

"She was mad and trying to cause strife. She probably didn't mean it."

Missy was horrible to him, and he was kind

enough to extend grace when it wasn't deserved. He really was a special man.

"Well, I don't agree with her. I can't believe she was so hateful. I feel like I really saw her for the first time tonight. She could be so sweet and kind, but I'm wondering if she did those charity things with me just to placate me and keep me going along with all the things she wanted me to do." The soothing motion of his hand rubbing up and down her back made her melt into him even more.

"I'm sorry, Ivy. I don't know. I will say I don't like how she's treated you. I couldn't understand her saying she cared and then giving you so many hoops to jump through. I could see you were struggling, and I've not known you as long."

Ivy lifted her gaze to his. "You've been so kind to me. I dragged you all over Seattle, and you never once complained."

"Oh, well, I think anyone that gets the chance to spend time with you should thank their lucky stars. What, with you being so pretty and smart." His eyes widened. "Uh, I meant…you know, people."

She tried not to smile, but the harder she tried, the more it formed. "I'll pretend I didn't hear that if it'll make you feel better."

His cheeks turned a scrumptious shade of red. "I'd

appreciate that." He rubbed her arms. "Would you like me to get you out of here? To take you home?"

"I'll have to book us a flight."

"Nah, I can fly us."

Her mouth dropped open. "You're a pilot?"

Kolby dropped his gaze to the floor like he was embarrassed. "Yeah, but it's no big thing."

"It's huge. That's not exactly a talent everyone has." The sweet unassuming man was so much more than he let on. Warm, gentle, and intelligent.

"Aw, nah," he said and smiled. "You give me an hour or so, and I'll have a plane ready for us."

Ivy's heart soared. "You'd do that for me?"

He nodded. "I think it'll do you good to get home."

"Nashville?"

"No, home." He smiled.

She sucked in a sharp breath. "You'd fly me to Gatlinburg?"

"That's where you're from, right?"

Tears stung her eyes. "Yeah." She threw her arms around his neck. "Kolby, you have no idea what this means to me. Thank you."

He hugged her. "We'll be stopping for fuel a few times, but we should be there sometime tomorrow."

"That's okay. I'll take it."

"Why don't you take some time while I get it

arranged and get some rest? I'll wake you when we're ready to go, and we can grab some supper on the way to the airport."

Ivy couldn't believe it. She was going home. It had been forever, and she didn't even live that far from Gatlinburg. "Kolby, how are you flying into Gatlinburg? It doesn't have an airport."

"I'm sure someone there has a private strip. If not, we'll fly in wherever, and I'll drive you there."

Her heart swelled. "Okay." She hugged him again. "You've been a blessing to me, Kolby. More than you'll ever know." She released him and stepped back.

Oh, how she loved his blush. Those beautifully tanned cheeks flaming red and that little lift at one corner of his lips. Such boyish charm and sweetness. Maybe if she abandoned her career, the stalker would go away. Then Kolby wouldn't be her bodyguard, and she could kiss him until her lips fell off. It was certainly a goal worth shooting for.

Kolby took her luggage to the bedroom, and she followed him in. "I'll see you in a bit," he said and winked as he shut the door.

Ivy walked to the bed and lowered herself onto the edge. The day had started so early. It almost felt as if she'd had two days in one. When she'd first walked into the room, she'd thought she'd jump in the shower before taking a nap, but now she wasn't sure she could stand up.

Scooting back on the bed, she rolled to her side and curled up. The bed was squishy, and it smelled so good. Not as good as Kolby. Nothing would ever smell as good as him. Not even her grandma's fudge brownies. The thought made her pause. That was pushing it. Her grandma's brownies were mouth-watering, and the smell was enough to pull you from a mile away. Ivy would call it a tie.

The one good thing about all of this was that she'd stood up for herself. She'd taken charge of her life again, and she was setting the ground rules for how things would be from now on. There'd be no more running over the top of her, pushing her to do things she didn't want to do, or running her so ragged she felt brittle.

That part of her life was over. If she decided she wanted to stay at the radio station, it would be her decision, and it would be because she wanted it. Not because someone talked her into it. Going home was going to give her the chance to get some perspective and find herself. Who was Ivy Manning, and what did she really want out of life?

Well, she did want to be successful. She wanted love. She wanted balance between the two. And as she lay there, she also realized she wanted to see if there could be something between her and Kolby. She liked him. More than liked him. Bodyguard or not, there was something there, and she could feel it. How could she convince him to give them a shot?

CHAPTER 9

"This is so cool," Ivy said, bouncing in the plane's passenger seat. "I've never done this before. Well, flying, sure, but not like this."

During the time it took Kolby to set up the rental, he'd wondered if maybe he'd made a mistake. Not just because it would put him in such close quarters with Ivy, but the time was a consideration too. It was a lot of alone time for a fella already struggling with attraction to the pretty woman he was guarding.

It hadn't taken long for Ryder to find a place that had a small plane available for rent, to get a background check, and then for Kolby to do a pre-flight check. The eerie feeling he'd had on the flight over had been for nothing, or so it seemed. Now that he was the guy flying, the little voice had all but put a sock in it.

The sun was setting when they took off from Bellingham, an hour and a half north of Seattle, and they'd be flying over the mountains in just a few moments. He glanced at Ivy, whose smile was nearly a substitute for the midday sun. It made his heart glad to see her so at ease.

"We'll be flying at night, so there won't be much to see soon."

"That's okay. I've got you in a confined space, and I have a list of questions a mile long. I think I can keep myself occupied." She smiled.

He flicked his gaze in her direction. Confined space? A long list of questions? Just what sort of trouble had he volunteered for? "Questions?" His voice rose an octave.

Ivy chuckled. "Are you scared?"

"Well, no. Not scared. Why do you want to know about me?"

"I'd like to know who's guarding me."

Heaven help him. "Uh, Ivy, I don't know if that's such a good idea."

She twisted in the seat a little and faced him. "Yeah, but you'll answer me. Won't ya?"

Well, she had him there. Resisting her charm was hard enough when there was a little more space between them. This tiny box with her sitting right next to him would make it impossible. "Yeah, I probably will."

"Where did you grow up?" asked Ivy.

"The hills of Kentucky. A little town called Livermore."

She crossed her arms over her chest. "I've met people from Kentucky, but no one ever had an accent as thick as yours."

"I had a speech problem when I was a kid. Some of it comes from that."

"Well, as I've said, I think it's a beautiful accent."

It was a good thing it was getting dark. If she was going to be tossing compliments at him, he'd need the cover of darkness to hide his blushing. He was sure she was just being nice. "Aw, nah."

"I see you blushing over there. I think I might just have to find a way to keep that color in your cheeks 'cause you're so cute."

"Ivy…" He shook his head, trying to keep the smile from his lips and failing. It made him feel out of sorts when she said stuff like that.

She giggled. "Flustered makes you even cuter."

The woman was killing him. He was already fighting an attraction to her, and here she was, flirting like nobody's business. How was a man supposed to resist her? "Well, you're as pretty as a picture. I've never seen a woman with eyes as brown and soulful as yours. The way you walk into a room is like a lighthouse that's picked up its foundation and sauntered in. And I bet your skin is as soft as a rose petal." Two could play at that blushing game.

When she didn't come back with anything, he spared a quick glance. Her expression was blank, and she was blinking.

"You really think all that about me?" she asked just above a whisper.

"Aw, sure, haven't you been told that plenty of times?"

She shook her head. "No."

"I'm sorry. You were making me blush, and I thought I'd throw a snowball in your direction."

Ivy leaned over and kissed his cheek. "That's the sweetest, most flattering thing anyone has ever said to me. You're quite the man, Kolby Rutherford." She sniffed and wiped her face.

Shoot. He hadn't meant to make her all teary. "I didn't mean to make you cry."

"Not all tears are sad. Some are...for joy. Thank you for that."

"I don't lie...well, except when you asked about my phone call. I just didn't tell you then 'cause you were hurtin' so bad."

She narrowed her eyes. "You *were* trying to get out of being my bodyguard."

He raked his hand through his hair. "Ivy, I just—"

A flash of lightning lit up the sky, and Kolby concentrated on the sky in front of them. When he'd checked the weather, it had been clear skies. Then again, he was flying them over mountains, and the weather could quickly change, especially in the spring.

"Is something wrong?" Ivy asked.

"Just a storm, but don't worry…" His voice trailed off as thick clouds loomed on the horizon and lightning flashed. "Uh, you don't have to worry, but you do need to hang on. We're approaching a storm. It wasn't on the forecast, but in the mountains, they can pop up pretty quick. The GPS will keep us straight, though."

Ivy gripped the chair arms. "Okay."

The fear in her eyes cut him to the quick. He cupped her cheek. "I will die before I let anything happen to you, Ivy. If something happens, I'll get us out of these mountains. I promise." He prayed that God wouldn't make him a liar. That He'd guide Kolby's hands and get them through the storm safely.

A large bolt of lightning streaked across the sky, spreading like fingers on a hand. A second later, a deafening crack shook the plane, and the instrument panel died. He gripped the wheel tighter as he tried to control the plane. "I'm going to have to land the plane."

"What happened?" asked Ivy.

Kolby's heart raced. He didn't want to scare her, but he couldn't lie either. "I think we were just struck by lightning."

"Lightning?" She squeaked. "But how will you land without crashing?"

He smiled. "I'm a good pilot." He was hoping he could ease her fears.

"What will happen if they don't find us?"

He gave her a quick glance. "We'll be okay. That's why I packed that gear. I had a weird feeling before we left, but since nothing happened on the way here, I shrugged it off. Guess I was right. Just wish I wasn't the cause."

She touched his arm. "It's not your fault lightning hit the plane. You couldn't predict that."

It didn't help the way he was feeling. Picking up the headset, he tried the mic, knowing in his heart that it was as dead as the rest of the instruments. "Nothing."

Her lips parted in a gasp. "So you can't tell anyone where we are?"

"No, but we'll be okay. There's enough gear to keep us warm. And you packed warm clothes, right?"

She nodded and grabbed the seat's arms. "My heart's beating so fast."

"Mine too, but we'll be okay." He paused. "Once we land, we're covered as far as warmth. And for food, it's spring, so there should be a few things we can gather up. Plus, there's fresh streams and fish, and I packed protein bars. We just need to stay dry, and we'll be fine."

Ahead of him, a narrow strip lined with trees seemed to be his best bet. It would total the plane, but other than being shaken up, he and Ivy would be okay. He tipped the nose of the plane down, shooting for the narrow strip, when a burst of wind knocked the plane sideways.

Ivy screamed, and Kolby struggled to get control of the plane. "Hold on, Ivy."

He tightened his grip on the yoke and looked for the small narrow strip again. He'd been knocked off course. Now he needed to find another spot to land. In the last bit of light, he searched the terrain, finally eyeing a space that seemed even narrower than the one before.

Pointing the nose down, he headed for the little strip because another gust of wind could hit. The plane bounced, and metal crunched as the wings hit the trees. He hit the brakes hard, hoping to slow it down before they hit the thicker part of the forest.

After what felt like hours but was probably less than a minute, the plane jerked to a stop. For just a moment, he allowed himself to breathe a sigh of relief. He'd landed the plane. Thank God, he'd landed the plane.

Now he had to make sure he got Ivy off the mountain as quickly as he could.

"Ivy?" Kolby's voice broke through the fog.

Plane crash. That's what had happened. "Kolby?"

"Yeah. You okay?"

She was sore from all the jostling, but as she took a quick assessment of herself, she realized nothing was broken. She leaned her head against the seat and closed her eyes. "I think so. Are you okay?"

"My head hurts, but I think I'm okay."

There was a click of a seatbelt, and she felt large warm hands cupping her face. "Ivy? Are you sure you're okay? You could be in shock."

She peeled her eyes open. Her gaze lifted to his, and his eyes bored into her. "I'm okay. Nothing feels broken or anything. I mean, I'm beat up a little from the landing, but I don't think I'd be any worse off if I'd been in a car accident."

Her vision cleared, and as he came into view, she could see he'd been cut. "But you aren't." She quickly unbuckled her seatbelt and touched his temple. "You're hurt."

"Aw, nah. I've had worse." His lips twitched into a half-smile. "As long as you're okay, I'm okay."

"Do those gear bags have a first aid kit?" In minutes, the sun would be down, plunging them into a black hole of darkness. If she was going to take care of that cut, it needed to be now.

"Sure."

She chewed her lip. "Would you let me take care of that cut?"

"Uh, okay, but it's fine. It's just giving me a headache is all. I promise I've suffered worse."

"Well, it'll make me feel better to know it can't get infected."

He hunched over as he walked into the belly of the plane, grabbed one of the bags, and sat with his back against the wall.

Ivy joined him by kneeling next to him as he pulled out the first aid kit. "When my little sister would skin her knee, she'd come to me before she would go to our momma."

"Is that right?" Holding her gaze, he leaned his head back.

"Mmmhmmm. I was the best at cleaning it out without making it sting too much." She pulled out some antiseptic, dotted a little on a small piece of gauze, and started cleaning his cut. He didn't so much as flinch. "Big tough Army Ranger guy not even making a noise."

Kolby chuckled. "I told you, I've suffered worse."

"Like what?"

He pulled his gaze from hers. "Oh, you don't need to hear about all that."

She unwrapped a bandage and placed it on the wound. "Maybe before we get off this mountain, you'll trust me enough to tell me."

Those steel-gray eyes lifted to hers, and she swallowed hard. "Maybe."

"We survived a plane crash," she said, the reality of what happened suddenly hitting her full force. Tears stung her eyes, and she circled her arms around his neck. "I've never been so scared. Even the stalker wasn't that scary."

Kolby wrapped his arms around her, his breath hitting her neck. And just like that, all her fears, anxiety, and stress were gone. He'd take care of her. He'd get them safely home.

"Thank you, God, for getting us on the ground without injury. Well, big injuries," he whispered so softly she almost didn't hear it.

"What did you say?" Ivy asked, leaning back, making sure she'd heard him right.

His cheeks turned pink as he released her and rubbed the back of his neck. "Just thanking God we made it safely."

She tilted her head and smiled. "So you do more than just say grace?"

He nodded. "Yeah, I do."

"Oh, okay." For some reason, it didn't surprise her. It felt good to know it because she believed in God too. Maybe getting lost in the mountains would give her a chance to find out what else they had in common and whatever thing he'd suffered. Not that she wanted to pry, but she wanted to know everything about him.

Inwardly, she lectured herself. They were lost, and she was trying to get cozy with her super attractive, muscled bodyguard. Wouldn't a late-night chat at her home have been a lot easier? In the back of her mind, a little voice whispered, *Probably not.*

He pulled out his phone and grumbled. "No signal, and there probably won't be one. This part of the Cascades is pretty remote." He looked around the interior of the plane. "Normally, I'd want to stay inside of it, but with it torn up like it is, I'm not sure it's safe in here. We'll camp next to the plane since the sun's already going down. I can make us a fire and find us some food to go with the protein bars I packed."

If she wasn't with Kolby, she'd be panicking, but he'd take care of her. "What do you want me to do?"

He smiled. "Do you know how to get a fire going?"

"Yep, I sure do." A shiver ran down her spine. "Oh, it's cold."

Kolby stepped into the back of the plane. "Here," he said, handing her luggage to her. You should put on the warm stuff you packed, along with the coat." He unzipped his duffle bag and pulled out his own coat.

While she put on her coat, he grabbed the two gear bags he'd packed and tried to open the door. It didn't budge. He tried again, and nothing.

"Door's jammed."

"What are we going to do?" Ivy asked.

He shot her a boyish grin. "Bust it down." And with that, he slammed his foot into the door over and over until it gave way. He pushed it with his hand. "Man, it's really jammed." Leaning his shoulder against it, his face turned red as he forced it open.

Suddenly, there was a pop, and the door swung open, throwing Kolby down to the ground. He sucked in a sharp breath and grabbed his arm as he sat up. "Oh, man. Gotta watch those rocks."

Darting out of the plane, Ivy kneeled next to him. "You okay?"

He rubbed his hand up and down his arm. "Yeah, it just smarts."

"You sure? You're not being macho, are you?"

A chuckle rumbled from him. "No, I'm okay." Looking up, he said, "Guess that updraft blew us out of the line of the storm. Looks like it's moving away too. At least that's something good." He pushed off the ground and helped her up. "I'll get the food. You get the fire started. Don't go far from the plane, okay?"

"I won't."

He winked and jogged to the edge of the trees. Oh mercy. That boyish charm coupled his sweet nature was a flame she couldn't seem to fight. How was she going to manage being stranded in the mountains with him? Especially when all she wanted to do was kiss him.

CHAPTER 10

*K*olby had returned from his foraging trip loaded with different berries and wild edible plants. While he manned the fire, he asked Ivy to step inside the plane and put on some more layers of clothes. Apparently, she hadn't dressed warm enough. The clothes she had on were okay, but she'd need more than one layer for an overnight in the mountains.

The air was so crisp and clean and pure. She didn't like being lost, but it was better than a wet jungle. It was so still and yet so alive at the same time because she knew there were things lurking in the dark that could eat her. It made her thankful she'd crashed with an ex-Army Ranger.

She'd been pleasantly surprised when he came back

with enough food that she found herself turning some of it down. "That wasn't nearly as bad as I was picturing it," she said, adjusting to get comfortable. The log he'd manhandled to the fire was an okay bench, but it wasn't meant for comfort as much as a place to sit while they ate a quick meal.

"What? The berries?" he asked.

Ivy shook her head. "No, the protein bars. Some of those things are downright disgusting."

Kolby laughed. "I'll give you that. Not the worst things I've eaten, but pretty far up there."

"Oh yeah? What's the worst thing you've ever eaten?" She had a story and a half. There was no way he could beat her.

"Rotten rice."

Ew. She could picture it. What was she thinking, asking such a stupid question? But she'd started it, and she wasn't a squeamish debutante.

Ivy squared her shoulders. "I was actually dared to eat an earthworm."

He tilted his head. "Is there a book about that?"

She leveled her eyes at him. "Where do you think the idiot got the idea?"

Kolby laughed. "You ate it. And you said your challenger wasn't the brightest?"

"No, smart aleck. When Peaches Weatherly throws down a dare, you gotta do it."

"Her name is Peaches?"

Ivy tipped her head toward him. "And let me tell you, that girl came from a rotten tree."

He nodded as he laughed. "Okay, so you ate a worm."

"I did, but it wasn't your typical worm."

His eyebrows knitted together. "What did she make you eat?"

"That hateful she-devil had me eat a red wiggler. It was the biggest, fattest, juiciest worm I'd ever seen in my life. She plopped that Godzilla of a worm down in front of me, and I turned green. But I ate it. I sucked that thing down like a string of spaghetti. Needless to say, Peaches didn't mess with me anymore."

Kolby held his stomach. "That's nasty, and I think it has more to do with the way you tell it than the actual event. No wonder you're so good at radio."

She tilted her head. "You think I'm good?"

"Of course I do. Just 'cause I'm silent don't mean I'm deaf. You give good advice, tell funny stories. People hang up happy when they get done talkin' to you. You pour light into the world with your words."

He thought that about her? *Her*? Oh, what a sweet

man. Now she was determined more than ever to learn all she could about him.

Glancing in his direction, she debated about what she wanted to ask him. The devilish part of her wanted to question him about not wanting to be her bodyguard since he didn't finish telling her about it before the crash, but she didn't feel it was the right time. She needed to be careful because she had a feeling Kolby was good at building impenetrable walls.

"So," she said, fanning her fingers in front of the fire. It was bright against the sheer blackness of the night due to the clouds. "Tell me about growing up in Kentucky."

He shrugged. "Oh, it was just like anywhere else. What about it do you want to know?"

"Well, do you have any siblings?"

"Nah, my momma had me, and there were complications. She couldn't have any more. By then, my dad wasn't in the picture."

"Aw, poor thing. That had to be hard."

He picked up a twig and broke it in his hands before tossing it into the fire. "I guess. She was really good to me until she met my stepdad."

"What changed?"

"Momma wanted things. Nice things. There was a rich real estate developer that blew through Livermore when I was about ten. They dated a little while, and the next thing I knew, we were moving to Lexington. I don't like to say I grew up there 'cause it gives me bad memories."

Ivy's throat tightened as she listened. "Was he mean to you or something?"

"I guess mean's the right word."

She moved over and covered his hand with hers. "You don't have to tell me any more, but if you want to, you can. It'll never go anywhere else."

"My buddy Noah is the only one who knows about my stepdad. For a long time, I couldn't talk about it, but we had to rely on each other during our last mission. You spend that kind of time with someone, and you end up telling them secrets you don't tell others."

Did that mean he was asking her not to pry any more about his stepdad? Maybe he needed to know he could count on her before divulging that kind of stuff. So, she switched gears. "What kind of mission?"

He cast his gaze to the ground. "I'll tell you that some other time."

"Okay." Ivy just wanted to keep him talking. "What made you decide you wanted to be in the Army?"

A smile played on his lips. "I wanted out of my house. Well, that was part of it. I wanted to go into the

Army and make a difference. Serve my country, protect people, do things I could be proud of."

"And I bet you did all of that. I mean, you still protect people, so I'm going to go out on a limb and say it's all true." Covering her mouth as she yawned, she shivered. "Is it getting colder to you?"

He nodded. "We should probably get some sleep. The day started early, and it was a long one."

"No kidding. That nap I had has worn off."

In minutes, Kolby had both their sleeping bags laid out, side by side about a foot apart. "Take whichever one you want," he said as he tossed a few more pieces of wood onto the fire.

She shimmied into one of the bags and zipped it up, and then he did the same. Her teeth chattered. "You're keeping the fire going?"

"It's banked, so it won't go anywhere while keeping us warm through the night," he said, his voice soft, like he was already drifting to sleep.

Ivy rolled onto her side, wishing she could see him. This whole foot-apart business was too far. She inch-wormed her way closer until she could kind of make out the shape of his face. God must have been hearing her gripe because the clouds parted to reveal the most beautiful moon and a sky full of glitter. "Oh, wow."

She looked over at Kolby sleeping soundly. Beauty

above her, beauty next to her. In that moment, she would've given a gold nickel to get the chance to run her fingers through his hair and across his cheeks. Would he sigh? Put his arm around her and pull her closer? Would he mumble something sweet in his sleep? What would it be like to press her back against his hard chest as his arms wrapped around her waist?

Her crush had hit the city limits of falling in love. She needed to slow her roll before she fell off a cliff. A crush was one thing, but the other? Missy wasn't far off about Ivy not needing a relationship. Her life was busy. Still...Kolby Rutherford. He wasn't the kind of man you just let slip through your fingers. He was the kind of man who would haunt you if you did. What should she do?

Nothing. They'd crashed on the side of a mountain, and her emotions were running high. That's all it was. Sure, her crush was still as present as before, but that didn't mean she needed to let it go any further. Besides, Missy was right. He'd move on as soon as Ivy's stalker was caught. She couldn't let herself get a broken heart by someone who'd be leaving soon.

KOLBY STOKED THE FIRE AS IVY EMERGED FROM HER

sleeping bag. He'd woken just as the sun was coming up, and it had given him the opportunity to grab them breakfast and get the fire going.

She stretched and covered her mouth as she yawned.

"Good morning," he said, marveling at how naturally beautiful she was. No makeup, no fancy perfume. Her hair mussed from sleep and her lips the perfect shade of pink. It wasn't fair that such a perfect woman was off-limits.

Yawning again, she said, "Good morning."

"Did you sleep okay?"

"Well, as far as beds go, I give it one star, but the peace and quiet bumps it to four." She smiled, and then it faltered as she blinked a few times. Her mouth dropped open. "The plane."

He twisted around. It was a total miracle they walked away alive. It was mangled. The wings were sheared off, and the body was crunched, with sharp pieces of metal sticking out here and there. "Yeah." God had heard his feeble prayers.

"We should be dead. The windows are all beat up. The wings are missing. I guess that praying worked." Her voice was soft.

"I guess so." He more than guessed. Waking up to

the mangled plane had him saying a few more prayers of thanks.

"How long have you been up?"

He squinted as he looked up. "I'd say about two hours."

"Why didn't you wake me up?"

Oh, he'd started to, unzipping her bag, finding her peaceful and sweet-looking. But he couldn't bring himself wake her up. The day before had been more than a hard day. "I thought you'd feel better if you got to sleep in. We'll be hiking all day, and that'll make you pretty tired. No point in getting worn down."

"Thank you. I do feel better. Sore, though." She reached a hand across her chest and rubbed her shoulder. "Man, I didn't think I'd be this sore."

He stood, walked to her, and crouched behind her. "That landing was rough. Your muscles are going to be sore for a bit." He set his hands on her shoulders and kneaded them, trying to ignore the zaps of electricity shooting into his arms and how delicate her shoulders felt under her clothes.

"Oh, Kolby. You sure you aren't a massage therapist?"

Laughing, he shook his head. "Nah."

She moaned long and low, leaning into his hands. "You can do that as long as you want." She let him continue a few more minutes before she said, "As much as I don't want you to stop, I guess I need to eat so we can get going, but, wow, don't be shocked if I ask for Kolby Rutherford's massage special."

"Come on, joker, and eat. Maybe we can get to a stream. We'll run out of water bottles soon and will need to fill our canteens."

"Yes, sir." She stood, and her feet got caught in the sleeping bag.

He caught her before she fell and held her to him. Man, he liked how she felt in his arms. She was so soft and warm. And those lips. He'd bet the farm they were as sweet as she was. "Uh, you okay?"

She nodded. "I'm okay. Thank you."

Her eyes were so sparkly. He loved that about her. The way her cheeks would rise as she smiled. And, boy, that little freckle in her hairline was waving a red flag in front of a bull. He so wanted to kiss it.

He'd promised he wouldn't leave, but by the time they got off this mountain, he might not have a choice. He couldn't fall in love with someone like Ivy Manning. Her friend Missy was right. He'd never be good enough for her. Not that he was a bad man, but she needed the finer things in life. A sophisticated man, not some dumb country boy with a too-thick Southern accent.

CHAPTER 11

With Kolby's long legs, it would have been easy for Ivy to get left behind, but he shortened his stride just for her. They'd been walking long enough that she was appreciative of his consideration too. Her calves were screaming for mercy. So much for those early morning workouts she was so proud of.

That massage he'd given her that morning was still sending her blood pressure to an unhealthy level. Good heavens and the stars above, the man had magic hands. Suddenly, her feet were aching to give them a go too.

"Ivy, do you need to rest?" Kolby's voice broke through her thoughts.

"What?"

"Your face is flushed. I want to make sure I'm not going too fast for you."

What could she say? It wasn't the exercise or the hiking; it was him? She'd had the best view while trailing behind him. He'd started the day with a coat, but he'd shucked it off, revealing a Henley that fit him like a glove. His back muscles would roll and move as he shifted and jumped over fallen trees.

Every time he took her hand to help her, she wanted to trip and fall onto his lips. If she didn't stop daydreaming about kissing him, she'd probably end up walking off a cliff. More than once, she'd nearly run into a tree. Her only saving grace was that she was behind him, so he didn't see her narrowly avoiding disaster.

"I'm…actually, I could use a break. I'm tired."

He smiled, the compassion rolling off of him in waves. "I figured so." He didn't walk another step, taking her gear off her shoulders and setting it on the forest floor as he let his drop to the ground. "Can't say I'm not a little weary myself."

Ivy trudged to a tree and sat down with her back against it. "My legs feel like gelatin."

"I'm sorry. I should have been paying better attention." His eyebrows knitted together as he walked to her and squatted. He cupped her jaw and rubbed his thumb across her cheek. "Your skin is getting a little chapped out here. Hold on. I'll get you something to eat and find something to help."

She was a strong, independent woman capable of taking care of herself. And she'd act like a baby if it meant Kolby Rutherford would take care of her. Actually, she'd do anything to just be held by him. It was so easy to picture. His arms around her, her head laid on his chest, and him kissing the top of her head. One of the most delicious daydreams she'd had. It was one that nearly had her headbutting a tree.

Kolby returned, handing her a protein bar and taking a seat facing her. He unscrewed a small tin, dabbed his finger in it, and smoothed it across her cheeks. By the time he was closing the tin, her heart was beating a million times a second.

"How's your head?" she asked, trying to force herself to focus on something other than the intense desire to kiss him.

He put his fingers to the bandage. "It's fine. Just a small headache today. Muscles are a little sore, but I'm as dandy as a fiddle."

Then she did it. Whatever switch she had for personal space was flicked off, and she combed her fingers through his hair. It just happened. He was there, and she was there, and *wham*. Fingers. In his hair.

His eyes widened, and she knew she should probably stop. But instead of yanking her hand back like a normal human being, she kept doing it.

He wasn't complaining. She certainly wasn't complaining. And it wasn't long before she was brushing the back of her hand across his jaw. The incredible moment continued as she cupped his cheek, his eyes slid closed, and he pressed his face into her hand. It was so special and intimate, and she'd never wanted anyone the way she wanted Kolby Rutherford.

But Missy was right about one thing. He'd be guarding someone else when they found her stalker. His job was dangerous. Could she handle watching his sweet smiling face leave, not knowing if she'd see it again? What if he got hurt? What if he was killed?

This tender bud of affection she had for him was powerful. How would she survive something even more consuming?

And as if he'd read her mind, he opened his eyes, his steel-gray silently trying to communicate something she couldn't read. If there was a sound being made, Ivy couldn't hear it over the pounding of her heart.

They sat there, staring into each other eyes for

heartbeat after heartbeat. Was this how souls became bound together? Holding each other's gazes, breathing in the other person's breath as invisible ribbon wrapped around you, sealing you that person? If so, she was pretty sure that had just happened.

Kolby cleared his throat. "I should let you eat," he said, his voice low and husky. Had he experienced it too?

Should she say something? Ask him? Would he pull away from her? Could she risk giving her heart to someone in his field of work? "You should eat too." It was the lamest thing she could've said, but loving Kolby could ruin her, and she wasn't sure she was ready for that.

KOLBY PULLED OUT HIS PHONE TO CHECK THE SIGNAL again as he leaned against the trunk of a tree, devouring his protein bar. Still no signal, just like he expected. Of course, that was his luck. Deep down he knew it had nothing to do with that, but he didn't want to be stranded with Ivy too long.

She was going to be his undoing. He'd applied salve to her cheeks. It was innocent enough. He was only taking care of her like he'd said he would.

Then she'd slipped her slender fingers into his hair, and his world had tilted on its axis. The feel of her fingers sliding through his hair, the way she brushed her hand along his jaw...words failed to truly capture how he felt.

He'd opened his eyes, and she was staring straight at him. Her perfect large brown eyes rooting him to the forest floor. His heart ticked faster and faster the longer she held his gaze. That's when it happened. The something he couldn't describe. The feeling that God had reached His hand down from the heavens, took his soul, and wrapped it so smack tight against Ivy's that Kolby thought he'd never breathe a single breath again.

What he couldn't understand was why God would do that to him. Why would He be so callous as to stitch his heart to hers when He knew Kolby couldn't do that? Even if her stalker was caught, there was the issue of his job. Would she want a man who was sent all over the world? His job was dangerous. He'd been shot at more times than he could count. Had the scars to prove that some of them hit the target. Would it be right to love someone so sweet as Ivy and put her through grief if something happened to him? He'd never be able to forgive himself if he brought her pain.

He could get a different job. Hadn't he said he did

it because it was something to do? Then again, he liked what he did. Helping people when they had nowhere else to go. And what was the point in even thinking about it? It wasn't like he had a chance with her.

It wasn't right or fair to Ivy either, so what was God playing at? Kolby knew God loved her too. Which made it that much more difficult to wrap his mind around. If He loved both of them, why would He put them in this position? Or Kolby could be a fool and think she was feeling for him what he was feeling for her when she wasn't. That was probably closer to the real truth. What on earth would Ivy Manning want with a backwoods Kentucky boy?

"Kolby?"

Her voice sliced through his thoughts, and he dropped his hand. "Uh, yeah?"

"I'm finished, and I think I'm ready to get moving again."

He popped the rest of his bar in his mouth and chugged some water. His belly wasn't near full, but the bar would last him until they made camp. "Yep, me too." Maybe pushing on would help him clear his head.

He gathered their trash and stuffed it in the side pocket of his bag. After he helped Ivy with her pack, he pulled his on. He covered his brow with his hands as he looked up. "Sun's not quite straight up. I'm hoping we can find a stream or river. Then we can follow it down off the mountain. Plus, we need some water. We've got two water bottles left."

"I'm following you." She smiled.

"How about I stay beside you? If you get tired, I'll notice quicker. Or you could just tell me." He glanced at her as they began walking. "Like before. You could have said you were tired."

She shrugged. "I really just don't want to slow us down."

He touched her arm, pulling her to a stop. "I'd rather be slower and know you're okay. You're not used to this, and it's easy to overextend yourself."

"I know, but we need water, and I can't imagine thirsting to death being the best way to go." She laughed.

He shook his head. "No, but there's no point in beating yourself ragged and still not getting there because you can't go any farther. We're in this together. Tell me if anything's wrong."

"Do you always care about people like this?"

His mouth lost all control, and words fell off his tongue so fast there was no catching them. He stepped into her, pushing her silky locks over her shoulder. "No, not like I care about you."

Her lips parted in a breathless gasp.

Soft and full. Ivy's lips were a siren's call. The hook that was her dug in further. Getting it out would cause more internal damage than he'd ever suffered. Moments like these were getting harder to resist, but he was a soldier. He could control himself.

He steeled his determination and stepped back. "We need water." And by the time they reached a body of water, he'd need a dip in it to cool off.

"You think they know we're missing yet?"

Change of subject. That's exactly what they needed. "I don't know. Probably. I mean, it's not like you aren't famous." He smiled.

Her lips pulled down, and she scoffed. "For once, it's coming in handy."

"Stop that. Two weeks after I took this job, you raised money for a homeless shelter. Not only did you serve them food, but you were the reason other celebrities showed up and donated. And you talked to those homeless people like their presence was needed and wanted. That meant the world to those folks. You could see it in their faces. You should be proud of your success. God's using it for special things."

"You think so?"

"I know so. I've witnessed it."

In a flash, she kissed him on the cheek. "You may not be famous, Kolby Rutherford, but you're being used for special things too." With that, she walked ahead of him, a new spring in her step.

He covered the spot where she kissed him with his hand, and all he could think was that if her real kisses were as incredible as her tiny kisses, his socks would be on the moon.

CHAPTER 12

Twigs snapped under Kolby's feet as they walked. "Tell me about your family," he asked.

Ivy smiled. "Well, I have two older brothers and a younger sister. My mom and dad were high school sweethearts, homecoming king and queen. Let me tell you, trying to live up to their legend was hard. Momma was smart, got straight A's. Daddy was captain of the football team. And from what I've learned, they're still just as much in love today as they were back then."

"That must be nice."

She shrugged. "It was, actually. I'd thought I was following in their footsteps. My high school sweetheart was the love of my life. I thought for sure we'd get married and have a life that mirrored my parents."

Kolby glanced at her. "What happened?" He couldn't fathom a man dumb enough to let Ivy go.

"Well, we were supposed to go to prom together, but I got strep two days before. I tried everything to get over it, but I was sick as a dog. I could barely hold my head up. I can't remember a time I was any sicker than I was my senior year." She sighed. "I thought for sure Greg would stay with me, but it was his senior prom too, and he didn't want to miss it. I really couldn't blame him."

"He went without you?" That blew Kolby away. No way would he have gone to anything like that without her.

Ivy nodded. "That wasn't the worst thing. A few days later, pictures started surfacing of him and one of the girls on the cheer squad kissing. Broke my heart. He apologized profusely, but I couldn't get those images out of my mind."

"What an idiot. Did you go back out with him anyway?"

Nodding, she said, "I tried giving him a second chance, but at graduation, I broke up with him. He tried again to apologize, but the damage was done. I couldn't look at him without seeing his lips on another girl. I want someone who wants me and no one else. So much so that the very idea of kissing another person makes them sick. Because that's how I plan to love someone."

Oh, to be loved like that. It was the way he wanted to love someone. Too bad it couldn't be Ivy, but he wasn't about to let that little thought take hold. Ivy was off-limits. "Yeah, that's how I feel too. When I give my heart to someone, that'll be it. Done and over."

"How about you? You can't tell me you didn't have a high school sweetheart."

He shook his head. "Nah, I was pretty shy in school. I kept to myself."

Ivy cocked an eyebrow. "As cute as you are, I *know* girls had to be crushing on you."

His cheeks warmed from the compliment. "If they were, I didn't know about it." Dipping his gaze to the ground, he said, "My stepdad was pretty rough. I didn't want to bring a girl home to that."

She quietly slipped her hand into his.

He gathered some courage. For some crazy reason, he wanted Ivy to know about his stepdad. He wanted her to know all his hidden parts, or at least as much as he could share until he lost his courage.

He took a deep breath and let it out. "He beat me a lot. So much that I sometimes wondered if he didn't marry my momma just so he could whoop me at his leisure."

"Your mom didn't stop him?" Her voice rose an octave.

"Nah, she looked the other way. I think she hated me for making it to where she couldn't have more kids." That thought had come to him when he was lying in the cage in Nigeria, waiting to die. It gave him the ability to extend grace to his mom and forgive her after all those years.

"Kolby..."

His throat tightened as memories of his childhood surfaced.

"Couldn't you run away or tell someone?" Ivy asked.

He shook his head, working to keep the emotions from showing on his face. "I tried once, but I found out real quick that adults couldn't be trusted. He'd always hold me down as he beat me, but when he found out I told, I thought he was going to kill me. After that, I kept my mouth shut."

"I...I don't have words. Where is he now?"

"In Lexington. Last I heard, he was being given some lifetime award. No doubt Momma was right there on his arm, proud as a peacock." He silently spoke forgiveness over his mom. Sometimes when he talked about things, it was easy to pick that anger back up.

Ivy stopped walking, jerking him to a standstill. "You need to tell on him. Someone like him shouldn't be living a good life. Not as horrible as he is."

He smiled. "The memories hurt, but I forgave him. Same with Momma."

She tilted her head. "How could you forgive him of something that awful?"

Still holding her hand, he stepped closer. "It wasn't for him. It was for me. Living with him, being beat by him, taught me that I don't want to be that kind of man."

"You're a better person than me."

"Nah, we just have different circumstances."

Her eyebrows knitted together. "How do you do that? Forgive someone that hurt you so badly?"

Kolby shrugged. "I had to decide who I wanted to be. Did I let anger turn me into him, or let it go? I chose to let it go. I never want to be the kind of man who strikes another out of anger."

Ivy stepped closer and kissed his cheek. "You are, without a doubt, one of the best people I've ever known."

"Aw, nah. There are much better people out there than me."

"And humble too."

He chuckled. "I wasn't trying to be humble."

"I think that's the very definition of humble." With her hand balled in his shirt, she leaned back, smiling. "I've never met anyone like you."

Casting his gaze down, he said, "I don't know what to say to that."

Her fingertips skated across his forehead, down the side of his face, and along his jaw. With one finger under his chin, she tipped his face up. She brought her lips closer, hesitated just a second, and then touched them to his.

Sweeter than candy, and he wanted more. "Ivy, I'm afraid I might disappoint you. I've not kissed many women."

Not a word left her lips as she pressed them to his again. A slow-burning fire built in his belly as her lips moved against his, each little kiss so tender and soft. With the last brush of her lips, she leaned back.

"I probably shouldn't have done that," she said. "I'm sorry."

He'd literally been tortured in the past, but in that moment, he'd never felt more wounded in his life. "It's okay. I…well, we should get moving."

"That's a good idea." She stepped back and began walking.

Kolby picked up the pieces of his heart and followed her. Missy was right, and it had taken a short minute for Ivy to figure out he wasn't good enough for her. The ache that settled into his marrow cast a cloud over him. He'd promised to protect her, and he would. He'd promised he'd stay her bodyguard, and he would. But he never said he wouldn't beg her to release him from those promises. When they got off this mountain, he was going to do just that.

Sure, he could and would protect her to the best of his ability if she didn't release him, but when it was all over, he could see his heart being in much the same condition as his body after being held prisoner. Broken and left for dead.

IVY TOUCHED HER FINGERS TO HER LIPS FOR THE umpteenth time as they walked along a ledge. They sizzled with the memory of Kolby's kiss. It hadn't been a deep one, but it had rocked her to her core. The best kiss she'd ever had, and it was little kisses. What would happen if she shared a real kiss with him?

When she pulled back and apologized for kissing him, he'd been quick to mask the hurt, but not quick enough. She could see the pain she'd caused him. It didn't hit her until a few moments later that he'd confessed he hadn't kissed many women. Kissing him had scared her. His job was dangerous, and she could see her heart being broken if something happened to him.

He probably thought she was pulling away because he was a bad kisser, and nothing could be further from the truth. She sighed. It was too late to tell him that. He'd never believe her. Oh, he would pretend he did, but a person couldn't say things like that and reel them back in, thinking they hadn't done damage. She'd have to prove it wasn't true by kissing him again, and she wasn't positive she could. Not without losing her heart.

"You hear that?" He tapped her on the arm.

A whooshing sound echoed in the distance. "Water?"

"Yeah, it's making me thirsty." He smiled.

She nodded. "Yeah, a nice cold drink of fresh water sounds good." Maybe a dip in it would be good for her. "I—"

Ivy yelped as the ground gave way under her feet.

Kolby grabbed her to keep her from falling. He inched back from the edge and settled his hands on her hips. "You're okay. I've gotcha."

They'd been inching their way on a narrow ledge.

Kolby had tried to find another route, but the other way was steep, making it even worse.

She held on to his arms. "Thank you. That was—"

No sooner had she said it than the ground gave way again. As she screamed, he threw his arms around her, and they slid down the side of the mountain. He tucked her head under his chin and grunted as they bounced and then landed hard. In what seemed like seconds, they hit the bottom and rolled to a stop.

Ivy lay there a second, getting her bearings. She lifted her head and couldn't believe how far they'd fallen. It was a wonder neither of them was in a broken heap. As soon as she thought it, she scrambled away from Kolby.

His eyes were closed, and she nearly swallowed her tongue. "Kolby?" She took his face in her hands. "Oh, please don't be hurt."

Grunting, he held his head as he sat up. "Never been on a roller coaster ride that good before." He shot her a cute half-smile. "You okay?"

She blinked back tears. "Yeah, I'm fine. Are you?"

"I think so." He flexed his arms and legs. "Yeah, no broken bones. Can't say my pack fared as well. One of the straps broke."

He started to push off the ground, and she gasped.

"Kolby, your back." He jumped as she touched him. "Your shirt's in shreds."

"It stings a little," he said, unzipping his bag. "Good thing I packed another shirt."

"Give me the first aid kit. I'll clean it up."

He glanced at her. "It's okay, really. It's just a scrape. I've had worse. The sting'll be gone soon enough."

Ivy knitted her eyebrows together. "It still needs to be cleaned." Holding out her hand for the first aid kit, she held his gaze. "Come on. I'm cleaning it."

"All right." He pulled out the first aid kit and handed it to her. Turning his back to her, he pulled his shirt off.

Ivy touched her hand to her mouth. She didn't have a single scratch, but his back was almost as bad as his ripped shirt. He'd taken the entire brunt of the fall. This was his job. The part that had her taking a step back. The man hadn't hesitated to spring into action to keep her from getting hurt. And he did this sort of thing on a daily basis—even after he'd felt rejected when she'd apologized for kissing him, or that's the impression she'd gotten from him.

"You really don't have to worry about it," he said.

She shook her head. "No, I'm cleaning it."

He drew his knees to his chest and wrapped his arms around them. "Okay."

Unzipping her bag, she dug out a shirt she'd stuffed in it. After dousing one of the sleeves with antiseptic, she gently wiped it across his back. Again, he didn't flinch. What had he been through to take what had to be extremely painful and just sit there, not saying a word?

As she continued cleaning it, his arms dropped to the ground. "I'm tired," he mumbled.

"I don't doubt you are. That fall was insane." She took another glance up the mountain. "I'm guessing you said a few prayers on our way down."

He chuckled. "Maybe a few."

"I'm finished."

Kolby just sat there.

"You sure you're okay?" Ivy asked.

He quickly pulled on his shirt, pushed off the ground, and nodded. "Yeah, I'm good."

Ivy put the kit away and stood. His eyes looked hazy. "I thought we needed to not push so we didn't get run down."

"I'm not. There's water not far from here. We'll set up camp, and I'll rest then." He smiled, shouldering his pack, and began walking.

Ivy hung back a step, watching him. He was

moving different. Not like he'd broken anything, but like he was sore and waving it off. Most likely to keep her from worrying.

She'd retreated from him because she wasn't sure she could handle loving a man like Kolby, but maybe she'd been too hasty. He was the kind of man women looked for their whole lives. Gentle, protective, and sweet. Here he was, right in front of her, and she was holding the very thing that made him desirable against him, that he was the kind of person who would take a job protecting people.

What did that say about her? Did she want to know the answer?

CHAPTER 13

"*I*t's getting louder. We have to be close now," Kolby said.

That tickled Ivy better than a feather. They'd been walking a long while according to the sun that inched into the trees. Her legs needed some downtime; otherwise, they'd turn into stumps. "Can't say I'm not happy to hear that."

"Yeah, I'm thirsty."

They'd finished off their last water bottle at least an hour ago, and Ivy's parched mouth was aching for something cold and wet. "Yeah."

Silence descended much the same as it had since she'd kissed him. He'd say a few words and then retreat again. No more chats or questions. She'd sure tried, too. He'd given one-word answers, no more than two. After a while, she'd stopped. She'd hurt him badly, and she couldn't blame him for not wanting to talk to her.

He'd shared a deep part of himself, and she'd basically told him he wasn't good enough. Not a good enough kisser and not a good enough man. Neither was true. If anything, she wasn't good enough for him. Someone so self-sacrificing that he'd take the pain of sliding down a mountain without complaint.

The sound of the water grew closer until they finally reached a rolling river. It wasn't big, but Ivy could tell it was a monster. She'd done a little studying of rivers when she was in school. These mountain streams looked safe, but they could drag a person under and make them a popsicle. And without a doubt, they were always deeper than they appeared.

"Those rocks on the edge are slick. Stay off of them. These rivers and streams aren't super deep, but the current is wicked, and the water is freezing. Unless you're a strong swimmer, it can yank you under and drown ya," he said.

Kolby unhooked his canteen and dropped his pack before trotting over to the edge and filling it. He brought it back to her and unclipped hers. "I have purification tablets, but I don't think we need them."

Again, he'd highlighted just how selfless he was. As

she took a gulp of cold water, she watched him fill the other canteen.

He stood, took a long drink, and walked back to her. "I'm going to go find some food and then try my hand at fishing. Mind taking care of the fire again?"

She tugged her pack off and let it drop to the ground. "No, I don't mind. I'll do a little fishing too."

Stretching his back, his eyebrows kneaded together. He sucked in a sharp breath and set his canteen down.

"Is your back hurting?"

He shook his head. "Nah, it's fine."

"Turn around and let me see."

He took a step back. She could practically see the wall he was building before he even opened his mouth. "No, Miss Ivy, it's fine."

"Miss Ivy?" she asked, barely able to find her voice.

"I think it's best if I maintain some distance." He raked his hand through his hair. "I know you think it makes you feel old, but it reminds me who you are and what I am. It'd do me good to keep that in the forefront of my mind."

Her mouth dropped open. "Distance? What?"

Kolby wouldn't look her in the eyes. "I think Missy was right, and for a second, I let myself think she wasn't."

"No, Kolby, I—"

Finally, he brought his gaze to hers, and they held such a depth of pain that she was at a loss for words. "Miss Ivy, I'm your bodyguard and nothing else. I can't be anything more than that. It's my fault that I let this go on, and you have my sincerest apologies. It won't happen again." He took off at a jog until he was lost from sight.

Ivy gawked after him. If the pain she was feeling was even a taste of what it would be like to lose him, she'd made the right call by pulling away. Then again, there was such a hole in her heart at the moment that a train could've driven through it. Which pain was worse?

KOLBY WAS GLAD THEY'D MADE IT TO A STREAM. IT GAVE him a chance to stop moving a second. Taking that fall down the mountain made Kolby sore. One minute they were standing there, and the next, he'd felt the earth give way and grabbed her. The next thing he knew, they were going down. It had hurt, too, and he knew he'd be feeling it for a few days. Luckily, he'd not broken anything.

Kolby flicked his homemade fishing pole and let

the line sink into the water. When he'd returned from finding some edibles in the forest, the fire was already going. He knew she was upset with him, though. Their conversations were minimal. A word here and there.

When she'd apologized for kissing him, it had cemented what he'd thought all along. Trying to be anything more than her bodyguard was stupid. Aside from his job, he wasn't cut out to be with someone like her. Missy was on to something, and maybe it had taken Ivy a second to realize she was right. Ivy was too good for him, and now she knew it too.

He'd hated putting a line between them, but it had to be done. Not only to protect his heart, but hers as well. Feelings couldn't get confusing if one of the parties wasn't participating. Besides, he'd seen the pity in her eyes as she apologized, and he wasn't a charity case.

A shriek came from Ivy, and she jumped up. "I think I caught something." Her makeshift pole bobbed.

"Hold on." He punched his pole into the rocky ground and raced to hers, grabbing the line and pulling it in hand over hand. Whatever was on it yanked, and the line sliced through his palm. He jerked back and shook his hands before grabbing the line again. He wrapped it around his hand, pulled as hard as he could, and a decent-sized fish broke the surface of the water, flopping as it hit the bank.

"It's huge," Ivy said.

It wasn't huge, but he'd let her think so. He picked the fish up by the mouth and looked it over. "This'll be a good dinner. Hold it a second, okay?"

She nodded. "Sure."

Once he had his hand cleaned and bandaged, he took the fish from her and got to work cleaning it. Of course, he wasn't going to eat any of it. It was just big enough that it might satisfy her. After he'd finished dressing it, he set it over the fire and went back to his own fishing pole.

She'd beamed at him, realizing she'd caught a fish, and all it did was make him want to see that smile every day for the rest of his life. He needed to get them down this mountain. This being alone together all the time wasn't working for him.

"I didn't know a man as big as you could fold up so small."

He jerked his gaze to her. "What?"

She smiled as she took a seat next to him. "Well, you had your knees to your chest, one arm around your legs, and your head resting on them."

Stretching out his legs in front of him, he nodded. "Oh."

Why did she have to sit by him? They'd barely spoken since he'd returned. He wanted to keep it that way. It kept him out of trouble.

"I expect you to eat some of my spoils of war."

Kolby shook his head. "Nah, I didn't catch it. Can't eat what you don't catch."

"If I share it, you can."

He shook his head. "No, you go ahead. I can hear your tummy growling."

She quickly slapped her hand over her stomach. "You heard that?"

"I think people in the Middle East heard that."

With a smack to his arm, she shook her head. "That wasn't nice."

He shrugged. "You're hungry. You can't help that."

"But you didn't have to point out that my stomach was growling."

"Not like you can hide it when it's wailing like a banshee."

She chuckled and cut a glance his way. "Fine, but you're sharing it with me."

"No, Miss Ivy, I won't."

"And stop calling me Miss Ivy."

He shook his head. He wasn't calling her Ivy. If he did that, it took away the degree of separation he needed. "No."

"You said you'd call me Ivy. And you have been. Nothing's changed that much that you can't keep calling me Ivy."

"It was a mistake to do that. You're my client, nothing more."

"You take that back right now."

What had gotten into her? "No."

"Yes. You take it back. Just because I kissed you doesn't mean you can't use my first name."

He stood, and she scrambled to her feet.

There was a fire in her eyes as she held his gaze. "My name is Ivy. Call me Ivy."

"I will not. I have to maintain some distance."

She glared at him. "Distance my foot."

He stepped to her. "I am your bodyguard. Not your friend. You need to get that through your head."

"Whether you like it or not, Kolby Rutherford, you are my friend. Once you crossed that line, it was done. You can't take it back. I won't let you."

He looked away and squeezed his eyes shut. God needed to get him out of this mess. His heart hurt, his back hurt, and he didn't know what to do. "Please stop," he said, working to keep his voice steady. "I don't want to argue with you. I'm too tired to watch my words, and I don't want to hurt you."

"Then don't. Just continue to call me Ivy."

Bringing his gaze back to hers, he sighed. "I...I just can't."

He stabbed his pole into the ground again, walked to his pack, shook out his sleeping bag, and slipped into it. "I'm right here if you need me, but I can't talk no more." He rolled onto his side, facing away from her.

"But you didn't eat anything."

"I'm not all that hungry anymore." It was a lie. He was hungry, but he'd manage. What he couldn't handle was talking to her. Couldn't she understand that it was hurting to put distance between them? He was doing it for her. To make it easier on her. That way she didn't have to feel bad about not wanting him.

A person couldn't kiss someone, apologize, and expect things to be the same. Did she really expect it to be that way? He couldn't work like that. Once he felt something, he felt it, and reeling those feelings back in was hard. And he was fighting himself to do what little he'd already done to put distance between them.

He felt a hand through his sleeping bag. "Kolby," she said softly. "You can't tell me you aren't hungry. You've got to be practically starving."

With a growl, he sat up, facing her. "I have first-hand experience with starvation. I can assure I'm not. Please, Miss Ivy, just..."

Her lips pinched into a tight line as she stood. "Fine. I'll leave you alone. I was just trying to take care of you the way you've taken care of me. But I'd hate to knock down a few feet of that wall you've so expertly built just so you can have a bite of food." She turned and then glanced over her shoulder down at him. "You want me to leave you alone? Well, I will. You want to be my bodyguard and only my bodyguard, then fine. You just go ahead and keep on calling me Miss Ivy. Like it changes anything."

She lifted her nose in the air, pranced to the fire, and sat down.

Again, he put his back to her. Finally, she'd gotten the message. Now they could both move on. Not that he would. That moment they'd shared earlier in the day had bound him to her. He'd make sure she was safe and taken care of for the rest of her life, even if it meant doing it from afar.

A few minutes later, he nearly broke down when he heard her crying. Oh, how he hated to hear her cry, especially knowing he was the source. He'd never wanted to be the cause of her tears, but what could he do? If he went to her, there was no way he could keep his distance. Not if she laid her head on his shoulder and sniffled just once. He'd be wanting to kiss her tears away, and after the disaster from earlier today, he couldn't risk it.

No, it was better to let her cry it out and not make her deal with him. After all, he was the one that got them into this mess in the first place.

As Kolby softly snored, Ivy stared up at the stars. She'd cried herself to sleep once already and then woke up again. For a tiny second, she'd considered striking out on her own, until the smarter part of her brain reminded her that sticking with Kolby was the better choice. Once that was settled, her thoughts drifted to their earlier exchange.

Her mind had never been in such chaos. It was a lie to say her heart wasn't already in trouble. Whether he left her alone, alive or not, Kolby's name was slowly being etched onto her heart, starting with that moment they'd shared. By her estimation, the cursive scrawl was halfway through the "L" in his name.

"I can't," Kolby murmured. "I can't get up." He

rolled onto his back, something she'd noticed he'd avoided until now. A tiny whimper escaped his lips, and he rolled onto his side, facing her.

He'd pulled on a beanie to cover his ears since she'd been asleep. She'd noticed she had one on too. How he'd managed to get it on and her not know was a mystery. Although, she had walked a long way. When she'd finally conked out, she was gone to the world.

She rolled to face him, thankful for the moon being so big and bright, allowing her to see him. With his hand curled under his chin, he took a deep breath, and his lips twisted like he was suffering. "No more. No more."

Was he dreaming about his stepdad? She couldn't imagine a little boy pleading with an adult to stop.

Kolby whimpered again and then rattled off his name, rank, and serial number.

He said he'd endured starvation. The only reason a soldier would give information like that was if…he'd been taken prisoner. A newfound respect bloomed in her chest. He'd suffered at the hands of his stepdad, chosen to serve in the military so he could help people, and then been tortured? It was just a guess, but it felt like the right one.

He gulped air as if he'd been held under water. "I

won't." He curled into a tight ball, shielding his head with his arm, and flinched.

Ivy's heart was breaking. She couldn't stand to witness him suffering, but she knew if she woke him up, he'd roll over and give her the cold shoulder. It was selfish as it could be, but the overwhelming need to hold and comfort him was more than she could take.

An idea hit her. She unzipped her bag, crawled over to him, and shook him. "Kolby, I think I heard a bear." She might've just been a radio jock, but she'd played a mean "tree number three" in a play when she was six.

Sitting straight up, he looked around, clearly only half-awake. "A bear?"

"Yeah, I don't see it, but I heard it."

He yawned. "It probably wasn't as close as you thought it was. You'll be okay now."

"Please let me stay with you," Ivy said, working her trembling lip as hard as she could.

Kolby rubbed his eyes and yawned again. He unzipped his bag and held it open for her. "Good thing these are oversized."

"Thank you." She jumped in, facing him, and lay down while he zipped it behind her. "We'll be warmer this way, huh?"

"Mmmhmmm."

The sleeping bag was oversized, but so was Kolby. It was a tight fit, but not so tight that she couldn't move a little. It didn't stop her body from being on fire where it smooshed against his.

He wrapped his arms around her, buried his face in her neck, and took a deep breath. "You smell good."

A smile grew on her lips as she pulled her arm free and stretched it across his back, careful not to touch the scrapes he had. She ran her hand back and forth across the space between his shoulder blades and pressed her face into his chest.

"That feels good," he said, his voice trailing off. Another deep breath, and she was certain he was sound asleep.

Ivy breathed him in. She smelled good? Oh, no. *He* smelled good. Masculine and woodsy from all the hiking. She could lay just like that forever. Just stay in his arms, pressed against him with his hot breath tickling her neck for the rest of her life.

Only, what happened when this job was over and he was guarding someone else? Would he live with them the way he lived with her? What happened when he was gone more than he was home? With her schedule, how would they ever see each other? His work took him all over the country. Her job took her all over the country. Would they grow distant for lack of time together?

The biggest question was, if by some chance they managed to make it work, how long would that life last? What was the time frame on forever when you were with someone who faced danger every day? How long would she have with him? One year? One month? Would she be one of those unfortunate brides to come home from her honeymoon, watch the love her life leave, and wake up the next day a widow?

How did the women who loved this kind of man not think themselves to death with worry? Most importantly, could she be the type of woman a man like Kolby needed? What if she wasn't strong enough for him? Missy was flat-out wrong. It wasn't Kolby who wasn't good enough for Ivy. It was Ivy who wasn't good enough for Kolby. What could she do to make herself good enough, and did she want that?

KOLBY COULDN'T REMEMBER A TIME HE'D BEEN SO comfortable and toasty warm. He was stiff but so well-rested. Normally, he was restless. Having been tortured, he had awful night terrors, and when they weren't waking him up, they were keeping him from sleeping deep.

Then he realized something...no *someone* had their back tight against his chest. Ivy. Her lithe body nestled next to his, her head resting on his bicep and her hair tickling his neck. His body was instantly aware of every spot she touched. Which, now that he was taking stock, was a lot of spots.

It came back in an instant. She'd thought she heard a bear, and he'd been a dope, offering to share his sleeping bag. She snuggled back against him further, stoking the fire that hadn't gone out. God was going to have to do him a solid and get him out of this mess.

Taking a deep breath, he inhaled her scent as his hold on her instinctively tightened. She was delicate and warm, and she filled him with a longing for more than he could ever have.

Turning in his arms, she let out a satisfied, peaceful breath.

He pushed her hair back from her neck and let his gaze rake over her face, marveling at God's work. Total perfection was encased in his arms.

He froze as she slid the tip of her nose up his neck, under his chin, and nuzzled his cheek. Did she know what she was doing? She'd kissed him, and he'd been bad at it. If he wasn't any good at kissing, he was even worse at the other stuff.

"Uh, Ivy. I mean, Miss Ivy…"

"You called me Ivy." Her husky voice tickled his ear.

"I didn't mean to. I just woke up and didn't have my bearings."

A smile twitched on her lips as she opened her eyes. "You mean to tell me a man who's trained to be on alert didn't have his bearings from the get-go?"

His sleeping bag had gone from toasty to roasty. "Uh, well, not when that man isn't used to waking up with a woman in his arms."

Ivy narrowed her eyes. "I find it hard to believe you've never woken up with a woman in your arms."

His whole body was inflamed. Couldn't God spare just small measure of mercy on him?

"You're blushing," Ivy said.

"Am not."

She cocked an eyebrow. "Really?"

"I don't want to talk about it. You'll make fun of me. People always do."

Her hand slid up his chest, and she rested it on his neck. "You should know me well enough by now to know I'd never make fun of you."

Hesitating, his set his gaze on the curve of her

shoulder. He couldn't bring himself to look her in the eyes. "I've never been...I've never done...I haven't been in love with anyone. I wanted to be in love when I did that."

"Are you saying I'm the only woman you've ever woken up with?"

He nodded, waiting for the laughter to start.

She hugged him around the neck, kissed his cheek, and smiled the widest smile there ever was. "That's not something to be ashamed of or embarrassed about. It's wonderful in my opinion. The only reason I'm not kissing you square on the mouth is because I've got morning breath, and I'm not that cruel."

If it wasn't already hot enough in the sleeping bag, now his face was on fire. "Aw, we should get going."

She giggled. "You're so cute when you blush."

Against his will, his lips stretched into a smile. "Miss Ivy, stop."

"And don't call me Miss Ivy, or I *will* kiss you on the mouth with my morning breath."

"Uh, that's not a threat."

She narrowed her eyes. "Don't tempt me, Kolby Rutherford."

He nodded, but never had he wanted to tempt someone so badly. Her kisses were addictive. Knowing he'd never have them again was painful. "Let's get going."

Ivy grimaced. "It's warm in here. I don't want to leave."

"Yeah, but we need to make some mileage. I'm never getting you off this mountain if we stay in this sleeping bag."

She caught her bottom lip in her teeth and smiled. "You make that sound like a bad thing."

If he didn't get himself out of that sleeping bag in the next five seconds, he was going to be kissing her, morning breath and all, good kisser or not. With a swift flick of his wrist, he pulled at the zipper, yanking it down.

"After you," he said.

She giggled. "You ever moved that fast before?"

Not even in a firefight, but no way was he telling her that. "Sure." A white lie was okay, right? He almost looked heavenward to ask. Almost. He didn't, though, because he was afraid of the answer, and he couldn't risk the truth.

Ivy slipped on her shoes and stood. "If you say so, but I have a feeling you're not telling the truth."

Kolby snatched his boots and stuffed his feet into them. He was either going to have to run his energy off or jump in the river to cool off, and the thought of an icy bath didn't appeal to him at all. "I'm gonna go get breakfast. My fishing pole is over there if you want to use it, or use yours or whatever. I gotta go."

He worked not to flat-out run away as he heard her light giggle behind him. She knew she'd flustered the dickens out of him, and it wasn't fair. He hit the second row of trees and turned on the juice, pounding feet against the ground until he was out of breath and panting. It had done nothing to quench wanting Ivy. All it did was make him tired, sweaty, and in need of a shower.

What was he going to do? It seemed as though she enjoyed making him miserable. Did she know how much he cared about her? Using her wiles like that on a helpless man. What had he ever done to her? So not fair. He didn't have any ammo to use against her.

His head was in such a whirl. Bracing his hand against a tree, he set his forehead against it. "God, I don't know what you've got up your sleeve, but this rabbit's about had it. She doesn't want me. Please stop making me hurt. I've hurt most of my life. Whatever I did, I'm sorry. Just please make it stop."

And like a joke, Kolby took a step, and his foot landed in a hole and twisted, taking him to the ground. Grunting, he grabbed his ankle and rolled onto his side. He couldn't understand all this misery. Why all of it was directed at him.

He took a deep breath, forced himself off the ground, and limped to a tree. How far had he run? Ivy was all alone. What if something hurt her? Once again, he'd been stupid.

"God, hate me all you want, but please keep her safe until I get back."

CHAPTER 15

*I*vy paced the campsite as she checked her phone. Not only was there no signal, but it was dead. Even if it hadn't been dead, she knew it wouldn't have a signal. Not up in these thick mountains.

Kolby wasn't back yet. He'd never taken this long. Had something happened to him? Is this what it would feel like to fret and worry and wonder if she'd ever see him smile again?

Chewing her thumb, she stopped and searched the area. She had half a mind to go looking for him, but getting lost would be stupid, and that's exactly what would happen. She was bony, but that didn't mean a bear wouldn't want to chew on her.

"Ivy," Kolby called.

She swept her gaze along the line of trees and found him holding on to the trunk of one. He laid his head against it. His shirt was darkened like he'd been sweating buckets. She broke into a run and slid to a stop as she reached him.

He pulled her into a bear hug. "Are you okay? You didn't get hurt while I was gone, did you?"

"I'm fine," she said and pulled back. His hair was matted to his head, and his face was pale. "But you aren't. What happened? Why were you gone so long?"

He took a long breath. "I was stupid. Stepped in a hole and twisted my ankle. I tried to get back as fast as I could, but the sprained ankle slowed me down." He took her face his hands. "But you're okay? Have you eaten?"

Ivy was dumbstruck. He was the one hurt. He was the one needing care, and his sole focus was her. What had she done to deserve a man like this? *Did* she deserve a man like this? All she'd done was slink away like a coward at the very thought of loving him.

"Yeah, I ate." She pulled his arm across her shoulders and hooked her fingers in one of the loops of his jeans. "You need to sit down."

With some effort, she got him seated on top of his sleeping bag. He was out of breath, and she could see the pained expression on his face.

"I saved you some food," she said as she unlaced his boot and pulled it and his sock off. His ankle was swollen, and a deep-purple bruise had already formed. "You sprained it pretty bad."

"I just need a little time off of it, and I'll be fine." He eased himself down on the sleeping bag. "Just a little rest."

Ivy walked to her pack, dug out the shirt she'd used to clean the scrape on his back, and took it to the river, dunking it until it was soaked. Once she had it wrung out, she went back to Kolby.

"Cold!" he yelped as she wrapped it around his ankle.

"It'll help with the swelling." She dragged his pack over and set it under his foot. "And this will too."

He nodded. "Could I bother you for some water?"

"Not a bother, Kolby," she said. She crawled to the canteen sitting not too far from them and pulled it over by the strap. Lifting on his elbow, he twisted the top off and drank until it was nearly dry.

Finally, he pushed it away. "I'm good." He eased himself down again. "Thank you."

Bracing her hand on the sleeping bag, she leaned over him. "I was worried about you."

"I'm sorry. I know I said I'd get you down the mountain. I promise I will."

Tears stung her eyes. "That's not what I meant. I meant I was worried about *you*. I pictured all sorts of horrible things."

"I'm so sorry."

She laid her head on his chest and closed her eyes, silently thanking God for each one of his heartbeats.

"I didn't mean to make you cry," he whispered.

Wiping her eyes, she sat up. "Not all tears are sad, remember?" She smiled. "You're exhausted. How far away did you go?"

His lashes fanned against his cheeks as he looked down. "I don't know. Far. I wasn't paying attention."

"I have a feeling that was my fault."

"Nah, it was mine. I was stupid." He took her hand and rubbed his thumb across the back of it. "I shouldn't have done it. I should've paid attention, watched where I was steppin'."

"Well, you can start eating with the bit I saved you, and I'll catch you another fish."

He shook his head. "You can't eat what you don't catch."

"I'm catching a fish, and you're eating it. I know you're hurting and hungry. Just because you're the bodyguard doesn't mean you don't need someone to take care of you sometimes."

He shrugged. "It's okay. I'll be fine. Really."

She set her palm flat against the sleeping bag next to his jaw. That ribbon tying her soul to his tightened a little more. Never in her life had she wanted to kiss someone so badly. No, *needed* to kiss someone.

Setting her cheek against his, she kissed the side of his face. Oh, there was that ribbon, lacing itself in and out, over and under. It tickled her heart, curling around it like it had fingers.

Pulling back just slightly, she nuzzled his jaw with the tip of her nose, bringing her lips closer to his.

The air around her was no longer crisp and chilly. It was so electrified that her skin felt scorched.

She brought her lips to his, tasting them. Light touch after light touch fueled the desire so heady and strong that they weren't enough to satisfy anymore.

Kolby had to be feeling the same way. He buried his hand in her hair, cupping the back of her head, and deepened the kiss as a soft moan rumbled from his throat.

She was ruined. Right then and there, she knew she was undone. Kolby Rutherford was all she'd ever want. The last scrap of ribbon weaved itself into a bow smack-dab in the middle of her heart. Together or apart, this man had her.

That niggling cowardly voice reared its ugly head. If she lost him, she'd be a shell until she was ashes. The sun could shine bright and bold a foot from her and not pierce the darkness she'd be plunged into. Could she gather enough courage to love him and risk being broken?

Slowly, the kiss ended with more light touches. She wasn't sure if she wanted to start it all over again or run so far away that she'd never find her way back. And she'd never been so out of breath and out of her mind all at once.

She opened her eyes, and his steel-grays were staring back at her. And like an alarm ending the best dream ever, his stomach growled.

"I think I'll go get you some more to eat," she said and laughed.

All he did was nod.

Pushing off the ground, she sauntered to the bank and grabbed her fishing pole, dug around for some bait, and plunked it in the water. She touched her fingers to her lips as tears rolled down her cheeks. Now she had to decide if she was a mouse or a woman. If she scampered away, she'd hurt both of them. If she planted her feet, there was a chance for a tsunami of grief.

Quietly, she murmured, "God, I don't pray much, but if you're listening, please help me. I don't want to get hurt, and I really don't want to hurt him. He's a good man. I'm not even sure why you'd send someone so great to me. Whatever did I do to earn enough favor that you'd give me someone as wonderful and caring as him? And how can I love him unselfishly?"

That was the rub. The key to all of it. *Was* she willing to love him unselfishly?

KOLBY KEPT HIS EYES TRAINED ON IVY AS SHE SAT BY THE river. His heart was still in his throat, beating wildly. He was positive it would never beat normal again. Whatever soul tie he had with her was taken to a new level.

She'd kissed him again. If they ever sent another craft to the moon, they'd actually find his socks. He didn't have much to compare it to, and truth be told, he was glad of that. She was the only woman he ever wanted to kiss again.

Apparently, he'd not done too bad this time. She didn't apologize, but then again, maybe she was saving his feelings. After she'd kissed him the last time, he'd taken to calling her Miss Ivy. She hated that, and perhaps she kept her disappointment to herself to keep that from happening again.

A squeal broke through his wondering, and Ivy

wrapped the line around the pole, reeling the fish in. Man, he should've been that smart. His hand wouldn't have a cut on it.

Once she had it out of the water, she trotted over to his pack, grabbed his knife, and pranced over to the spot where he'd cleaned her fish the day before.

She looked over her shoulder, a wide grin spreading from ear to ear. "It's bigger than yesterday's."

In no time at all, she had the fish cleaned and cooking over the fire. He was beyond impressed. "I didn't have to dress your fish yesterday, did I?"

Laughing, she shook her head. "No, but I didn't mind. It's gross. I usually leave that to my dad."

"Is he the one who taught you?"

"Yeah, he said a woman should know how to take care of herself. Plus, we went camping a lot when I was a kid. I think he got tired of cleaning fish all the time."

Kolby pushed up on his elbow and smiled. "He's right about a woman being able to take care of herself."

"Are you just saying that 'cause you're broken and hungry?" She grinned.

He laughed. "Well, maybe." He moved his hurt ankle and bit back a stab of pain. After all he'd been through, all the beatings and the torture, his ankle was the thing that brought him to his knees?

A moment later, Ivy was by him. "I hate that you're hurting."

"I'll be fine."

"Stop saying that. It's okay to hurt. I pretty much think you hung the moon."

Kolby lifted his gaze to hers. "What?"

She palmed the side of his face. "You are one of the best men I've ever known. I wondered why I felt so much peace the second you walked in my door, but you exude it. This quiet grace that I can't get enough of. You can hurt. Great men hurt. They just keep going, and you have. You can rest a minute, okay?"

"Uh…" He was without words. A lump formed in his throat as he fought back emotions. She thought that about him? The dumb country boy that no one could understand half the time? From the second he hurt his ankle, he thought God was bringing him pain and misery for no particular reason. But if he hadn't hurt his ankle, he and Ivy wouldn't be having this conversation. She probably wouldn't have kissed him again either.

Kolby had often wondered why God allowed his suffering, but maybe it was the suffering that made him who he was. Of course, that didn't keep him from thinking God was big enough to find a better method.

Ivy touched her cheek to his. "You are a sweet man, Kolby. A sweet, dear man. I'm thankful I know you."

That lump doubled in size. "Uh…" he managed to whisper.

Leaning back, she kissed his forehead. "Now, I'm going to see if that fish is done so you can eat."

He nodded and watched as she left him to go check on the food. His heart pounded out a plea in Morse code that somehow he'd be granted enough mercy to call her his. There was little hope, but that didn't seem to deter his pitiful petitions.

CHAPTER 16

*A*fter he'd eaten the fish Ivy cooked for him, Kolby had rested a bit, and they'd pulled up camp. It wasn't easy, but he'd been through worse. A little sprained ankle wasn't going to keep him from getting them down the mountain. He'd known, when they'd set out following the river down the mountain, that it would be difficult, but he'd not expected the rocky terrain they were encountering.

"I'm slowing us down," Kolby said. "But by now, someone is missing us. We'll be found soon." That had been a constant prayer in the back of his mind since he'd woken up that morning.

Ivy tightened her grip on his waist. "I think so too. I know Missy was mad at me. I mean, we've never been that angry with each other before, but we always cool down and work it out. I'm sure she's calling the National Guard by now."

"She was awfully angry. You were pretty upset too."

"I was, but I'm not anymore. I've known her so long, and I do love her. She's pushy because she has to be. The people she deals with can be a headache and a half, and they don't know how to take *no* for an answer. They've rubbed off on her, and she gets caught up in it. Plus, I've been a serious pushover and let her get away with too much. She forgets I have a say in it. But I'm not doing that show. I don't like Charla, and I don't want to move to Seattle. I like where I live. If my schedule could open up a little more and I could spend more time with my family, I'd be fine."

Kolby laughed. "I could tell you didn't like the show or Charla."

Ivy looked up at him. "Really? I was working hard to keep that fact off camera."

She couldn't have hidden that from him. He'd worked to get to know her and the things that bothered her. "You were forcing yourself to smile, and I could tell."

"I didn't even realize it."

"Aw, I bet no one else noticed. I'm sure you're fine." His gaze lowered to her lips.

She smiled and cut a glance his way. "How much have you been staring at my lips?"

He choked and stumbled, nearly bringing them both down. "You're gonna make us fall."

"That didn't answer my question."

"I haven't been," he said, and his gaze immediately dipped to her lips again. "I haven't."

Giggling, she said, "You just did it."

"We were talking about them. I couldn't help it. It was a reflexive thing."

Ivy laughed harder. "Have I told you how cute you are when you get flustered and blush?"

Kolby grinned as he looked away. "Aw, stop that." He wiped his arm across his forehead.

"Stop being so cute."

This woman was going to be the death of him. "Stop."

"You have pretty eyes, too."

He shook his head. Yep, someone somewhere was carving his tombstone. "Miss Ivy…" He held his breath as he realized what he'd said.

Ivy jerked them to a dead stop.

"What?" she asked, her eyebrows furrowed.

"Nothing."

"I distinctly heard you say Miss Ivy. We've

discussed this. No more Miss Ivy. I will leave you to rot on this mountain if you call me that again."

He smiled. "Nah, you wouldn't. You're the sweetest woman I've ever met."

She narrowed her eyes. "I can also be the angriest woman you've ever met. You wanna test me?"

With that look in her eyes? The fiery *I might hog-tie you first and then leave you to rot* look? He might not be the smartest guy on the planet, but he wasn't dumb enough to tick her off further. "No."

"Good boy," she said and smiled sweetly.

"You pet my head or hand me a treat, and I'll let you leave me on this mountain to rot," he grumbled.

She reached up and kissed him on the cheek. "That was a treat. You want to be left?"

The tips of his ears burned so badly they hurt. "No."

They started walking again, the silence stretching. She had to stop with all that cute stuff. And pretty eyes? They were just eyes. Unlike hers. Dark and twinkly. The kind a man could drown in and not complain when he was gasping for air.

After they'd walked a while longer, Kolby shielded his eyes as he looked up. The sun was halfway to the trees to the west, and with his current speed, they wouldn't get a whole lot farther before sunset.

He was especially grateful when the terrain transitioned back to dirt. Not only was it easier to walk on, but it would be easier to sleep on too. Plus, as much as he wanted to fight it, he was tired, and the idea of bedding down on rocks wasn't appealing.

As he set his pack down, he braced his hand on a tree, trying to catch his breath. He was a fit guy and worked out, yet traversing that rocky path with a sprained ankle had kicked his keister. Leaning his forehead against his arm, he closed his eyes and said a short prayer of thanks that they'd made it as far as they had.

"Kolby, are you okay?" Ivy asked.

With a smile, he lifted his head and nodded. "Yeah, I'm fine."

Her fingers brushed against his temple. How could such a small gesture hold so much comfort? "Your eyes tell a different story."

"My eyes?"

"They change color. Right now, they're a little dull." Stepping into him, she put her arms around him, her palms flat against the space between his shoulders. "You can lean on me. I promise I won't snap."

He was a soldier—big, tough, and made of steel. But at that moment, paper would have been stronger. It was weakness to feel that way. A man was supposed to take care of a woman. Not the other way around. Except, he couldn't shake the feeling that it was okay to be honest with her.

Wrapping his arms around her, he set his forehead on her shoulder and said, "Ivy, I absolutely hate admitting this, but I'm tired, and my ankle hurts."

She took a deep breath. "Will you let me take care you?"

"Yeah."

"I promise with all my heart that I'll never see you as anything other than a strong, protective Army Ranger. You're still my protector. You always will be."

He chuckled. It was a silly thing, but that little declaration did his heart good. She believed in him, even at his weakest. Something he'd been wanting for a long time. A woman to hold on to and to hold on to him, even in the midst of a storm. Only now, that woman had a name. Ivy. And just like the plant, she'd wrapped herself around him so strongly that he couldn't see breaking free. He didn't want to, either, because in her arms, he felt peace.

As Ivy fished, she glanced over her shoulder at Kolby. He was lying on his sleeping bag with his foot propped up again. She'd caught three fish already, and she was going for a fourth. He was going to have a full belly if it took her all night. She knew he had to be hungry. He'd barely eaten since they'd crashed. Well, barely eaten for a man his size.

His ankle didn't look great either. It was swollen to twice its normal size, and the dark purple-and-green bruise covered the bone in his ankle and spread around his heel. It wouldn't surprise her if he'd broken it. If nothing else, it went beyond a simple sprain. He'd torn something. She was sure of it.

"I've never seen a woman so determined to catch fish," he said.

They weren't as spread out as they were before, and they could camp far enough from the bank to be safe but close enough that they could have a conversation without yelling.

She shrugged. "I know you're hungry, and the fish are biting. Why not fill up tonight?"

"Aw, I'm not that hungry. You don't have to keep fishing."

"I need one more, and we'll both have two. I know I can eat at least one, maybe half of another, and you can have the rest. Food is strength, and you need yours."

He took a deep breath and rose up on his elbow. "Thank you."

She shot him a glance. "Is that you, Kolby Rutherford? I could have sworn you said thank you without putting up a fight."

Shaking his head, he smiled. "Aw, stop it."

Even from where she was, she could see him blushing. It never got old, either. He'd gotten flustered and called her Miss Ivy. She'd threatened to leave him on the mountain if he did it again. Inwardly, she was giggling up a storm because he was so cute, him telling her she was too sweet to do that. The little grumble only made him that much cuter. And the kiss on the cheek? His face was as red as a stop sign.

It was all great, but the best part was the hug he gave her. Laying his head on her shoulder and admitting he needed help. It meant he trusted her. She could feel it in the way he held her. That meant the world to her. It also scared her. He trusted her, which meant she could hurt him, and she didn't want to do that. She never had, but now she knew without a doubt that she held that power.

"Do you like to camp? You said your family went camping, but nothing about if you enjoyed it or not," he said, picking up a pine needle and twisting it around his finger.

She nodded. "I do. I loved it as a kid. Getting to explore and swim in the rivers and creeks. It was so much fun. Like I said, I went a lot as a kid. Did you do anything special?"

"Uh, not really. We were really poor. My mom worked three jobs. My nanna, my mom's mom, would babysit me. Man, I loved her. She'd make me cookies and read to me, and she had a way of hugging me that settled all my fears."

"Do you visit her often?"

"Nah, she passed some while ago. Actually, I didn't even know she'd passed. She didn't like my stepdad, and so she had a huge falling out with my mom. My mom wouldn't let me talk to her anymore. Right before I joined the Army, I went to visit her, and I learned she'd died months before. My mom never even tell me she was sick."

Ivy's lips parted. "You didn't get to visit with her before she died?"

He flicked a few leaves away. "No, and I was grieved that she died without me telling her I loved her one more time, but I'll get to see her again."

"I'm sorry. I bet that was hard."

"Aw, she knew I loved her, and I know she loved me." He smiled. "I miss her, though. The guys in my company had people to write home to, but I didn't. I wish I could've written to her."

She chewed her lip. "I know you said you don't visit your mom. You didn't try writing to her?"

"Oh, I tried once, but…" The sentence trailed off as his voice broke. He cleared his throat. "I told her I loved her and that I forgave her for letting my stepdad beat me. Part of the reason I don't go see her is because she called me a liar and said I was an ungrateful brat for not appreciating the life we had."

"That's awful. Kolby, I just don't have words. It's wrong."

Her line jerked, and she jumped to her feet. "Oh! Last fish! It feels big, too." It yanked hard again, and she leaned over, stepping closer and putting her foot on one of the moss-covered rocks.

"Ivy! No!" Kolby yelled.

It was too late. She could feel herself pitching forward. Her eyes widened. She could almost feel herself freezing to death in that water.

A heartbeat later, large hands grabbed her by the waist and pulled her back, her rear end hitting the dirt. "Don't—"

The sentence dropped as Kolby slipped and fell into the river. For the first time in her life, time seemed to stand still as she watched him hit the water.

A second later, his head broke the surface with a huge gasp a foot or so farther down, and just as fast, he was sucked back under.

Ivy ran down the bank. What was she going to do? Glancing around, she saw a broken tree limb that looked long enough for him to grab on to. She grunted as she picked it up and ran, hoping Kolby would pop up close enough for her to reach it out to him.

Moment after moment went by before his head popped up again another few feet down. She ran down the bank to catch up and stretched as she held it out to him. "Kolby! Grab on!"

His large fingers curled around the branch, and she pulled as hard as she could.

Finally, she managed to get him to the bank where she helped him out of the water. They tumbled to the ground and lay shoulder to shoulder.

She swung around, taking his face in her hands. "Kolby?"

He pulled away, choking and coughing up water. He gulped air several times before coughing more up.

"A-a-a-re y-oo-u ok-k-kay?" he asked between coughs. His teeth chattered, and it seemed as if he was fighting to ask the question.

She was fine, but he was going to have

hypothermia if she didn't do something quick. "We need to get you into a sleeping bag and get you warm."

Kolby curled onto his side, arms pulled tight against his body and fisted hands drawn over his stomach. He coughed again, and she noticed his ankle looked a little more bruised. She suspected he'd hit it while he was being dragged down the river.

With his sprained ankle, there was no way he could get back to camp. "I'll be right back. I need to get the sleeping bag and start a fire so your clothes can dry."

CHAPTER 17

*J*vy moved faster than she ever thought she could. She blistered a trail back to camp, grabbed Kolby's sleeping bag, and hurried back. She'd get him in the sleeping bag first and then gather wood for a fire.

Shaking out the sleeping bag, she leaned closer when she heard him mumbling and realized it was his name, rank, and serial number. He was saying it over and over. What had he been through?

"I'm here," she said as she put her arms around him and helped him sit up. "We need to get you out of those wet clothes and get you warm."

Together, they pulled his shirt off. It took a little more effort to get his jeans off, but she finally peeled them off and got him in the sleeping bag.

As she raced around gathering wood, the image of him stripped to his boxers stoked a fire in the pit of her stomach. If he wasn't freezing to death, she'd be tempted to take a picture of him and hang it on her wall. Wow. She'd known he was fit, that he was muscular, but his shirt hid a massive chest and incredible sculpted abs. And she was a horrible human being for even thinking it at a time like this.

"Nice, Ivy. He's freezing to death, and you're drooling over his body," she grumbled to herself as she built the fire.

Once the fire was going and she laid out his clothes, she stripped off her own clothes, got in the sleeping bag, and quickly zipped it behind her. She put her arm under his neck and wrapped herself around him.

"Hold on to me, okay?" she said.

His frosty fingers brushed her back, and she nearly yelped. It may as well have been icicles gliding across her skin.

"Th-th-thank y-you."

Setting her cheek against his, she whispered, "Can't have my favorite soldier turn into an ice cube."

A chuckle rumbled from his chest, followed by coughing and a groan. He was still shaking so badly, and she was at a loss as to how to help him. Hopefully, he'd get warm soon.

He coughed some more. "M-m-my ch-chest hu-rts."

"You were under the water long enough that I… was worried." She'd counted to what seemed a million before his head broke the water. Another few counts, and she might not be warming him up.

"G-g-got c-c-caught on s-s-someth-th-thing."

She ran her fingers through his wet hair. "You scared me to pieces. I don't know what I would have done if something had happened to you. And not just because you're my bodyguard either."

Now that she had a second where she wasn't in abject fear of seeing him drown, she had a moment to reflect on what had happened. She'd nearly fallen into the water, and he'd raced over on a sprained ankle to keep her from falling in. If he hadn't pushed her back, she'd have hit that water. She was a decent swimmer, but she didn't see herself having a fighting chance, as fast as it had been hauling Kolby downstream.

How had he managed to move so fast on that ankle? How much had it hurt to do what he did? All to keep her safe and warm. He'd risked drowning for her. She'd read stories about heroism and sacrifice, but she'd never been the recipient of that type of gift.

She bit back tears. He could have died, and it would have been because of her. As fast as he reached her, he hadn't even hesitated to spring into action. This man in her arms was the kind you held on to for dear life. You didn't think about tomorrow or what could happen, you loved him right then and there as hard as you could.

Squeezing him a little tighter, she willed him to be okay. Kolby Rutherford was her favorite person in the world, and she had no idea how she'd manage without him in her life.

Kolby had no idea how long it had taken him to stop shaking, but his skin burned as feeling began to return. His thoughts were still hazy, and his memory was pulled back to his time as a prisoner. "I've only been that cold once before." His voice was soft and low.

Ivy was flush against him, soft and warm. "I guess being a soldier, you probably have."

He nodded. "When I was tortured."

"We'll talk about that some other time. Are you feeling warm yet?"

"A little," he whispered, tightening his grip on her and burying his face in her neck. "My ankle hurts."

"You shouldn't have walked on it."

Kolby grunted. A clear picture of her leaned over the river and slipping played in his head. "Couldn't let you fall."

Her lips brushed against his cheek. "As fast as you got to me, you had to use your hurt ankle. I feel terrible."

"No. I needed to protect you...been through worse." His head began to clear just a little. "When my company was taken prisoner."

"Why don't you wait a little bit before telling me."

He shook his head. Typically, he kept this part of him hidden from everyone and it wasn't something he talked much about, but his heart was telling him to show it to Ivy. "I want to tell you." Sharing it with her felt like the right thing to do.

She sank her fingers into his hair, combing them through it. "It'll never leave my lips."

"I know." He paused a heartbeat before continuing. "This group of guerillas in Nigeria was trying to overthrow the government. We'd been sent in to help. They were taking young boys to fight with them and killing anyone who tried to stop them. We were told to stand down, but our CO said he couldn't. They weren't just taking little boys to fight in their army. They were taking little girls to sell to fund it."

"That's awful."

"Our CO said it was our choice, but he wasn't letting them take those kids. We went in and drove them off, but they later captured us during another fight."

Kolby's chest hurt where he'd swallowed some of the river water, and he coughed until his throat hurt. He let his voice rest a moment and began again. "Our government had negotiated to get us back, and at the last minute, they decided to keep my CO, Noah. I don't know why, but I had the strangest feeling I was supposed to stay with him."

Ivy squeezed him. "Did they just let you?"

He shook his head. "No," he whispered. "They were going to make me go, but I fought with one of the guards. They tackled me and knocked me out, and when I woke up, I was in the cage with Noah."

Her breath hit his cheek as she gasped. "Cage? What happened?"

"Negotiations broke down after they got the other guys out, and the guerillas got angry. They starved us. When they'd finally give us food, it was rotten. But we were so hungry that we'd eat it and be sick for days. It was during the wet season, and it can get cold there.

They'd tie us to stakes outside in the middle of the village as a warning to the village of what would happen if they resisted. We'd freeze all night long."

"How long were you held like that?" she asked with a shaky breath.

"A total of eight months. We were nearly bones when they found us, but Noah...he was sick. He'd caught pneumonia. I would hold him to keep him warm when they'd leave us outside."

"How did you escape?"

"Another company stumbled across us as they retook the village. We got back to the States, and when we were healthy enough to stand trial, we were dishonorably discharged, along with the rest of the company."

She kissed the side of his face. "I hate that any of you went through that." Setting her cheek against his, she said, "I especially hate it that you did. I've grown accustomed to you being with me."

His mind felt groggy now that he'd gotten all of that out. "I'm tired."

"You can rest, and I'll be here when you wake up. I promise."

Kolby nodded. He didn't have a choice. The pain in his ankle, the freezing water, and now the warmth of the sleeping bag were pulling him into darkness.

CHAPTER 18

The dream Kolby was experiencing had to be the best dream ever. Ivy was snuggled against him, all warm and soft. Her skin was touching his and lighting a fire deep in his gut. If he had to picture the rest of his life waking up like this, he'd never wake up again without a smile on his face.

It wasn't until she took a deep breath and wiggled that his eyes popped open. That's when he realized it wasn't a dream. Ivy was staring right back at him, and they were in their skivvies.

He squeezed his eyes shut. "I didn't see anything."

She laughed. "You were freezing. You needed body heat. What was I supposed to do?"

"Just what you did, but…" His face was on fire, but

it was hot in the sleeping bag too. Maybe she wouldn't notice how red his face was.

"Look at me."

"No."

She palmed his face. "Kolby. I'm no survivalist, but I know enough from my time camping with my family that you needed it."

He peeked one eye open. "I'm trying to be respectful."

"I know. But I've got on more than some women wear to the beach. Everything is covered. Just don't look down, and it'll be okay." She smiled. "I respect you too, you know?"

Opening his other eye, he nodded. His heart was hammering so loud he almost couldn't hear her. "I guess you're right. It's just...I've never..."

"I know. Just keep your eyes on mine."

He nodded. "Okay."

Her hand slid up his back, stopping on his shoulder blade. "How are you feeling?"

The moment made it difficult to concentrate on things other than kissing her, but he did what she said and trained his gaze on hers. "I think I'm okay. My ankle isn't."

She nodded. "Yeah, I didn't think it would be, but it

was more important to get you warm. Your clothes should be close to dry by now."

"How long was I out?"

"A few hours."

His jaw dropped. "You stayed the whole time?"

"Yeah, it would have been you pulling me out of that cold water if you hadn't come to the rescue. And from what I could tell, that water was way faster than I could've handled. You saved my life. Spending a few hours making sure you were okay seemed rather small in comparison."

It was his job to save her life, but it had moved beyond job and more toward desperation because a world without Ivy wasn't a world he wanted to be in.

"I know it's your job, but it doesn't make it less heroic." She smiled.

Should he correct her? What did Kolby Rutherford have that someone as refined and smart and beautiful as Ivy Manning could want? He hugged her to him. "I saw you about to fall. I saw you hitting that water and never coming back up. I couldn't let it happen. I don't even remember running to you."

"Hence the heroic part." She chuckled.

"I wasn't trying to be. I was doing my job." He knew the moment it left his lips that it was the wrong thing to say, and he hadn't meant it like that.

Her body went stiff in his arms. "Right. Your job."

"I didn't—"

"Would you close your eyes? I need to get dressed." She pulled away and shut him out in a blink.

"Ivy, I didn't—"

She held up her hand. "Stop. Believe me, it's really easy to want this to be more than what it is, but the truth is, your job is dangerous. I'm not cut out for that."

He nodded. Working to keep the emotion out of his voice, he said, "Oh, yeah, I just meant I like protecting you. It doesn't feel like just a job."

She smiled. "Well, see, this is good. So, let me get dressed, and I'll get dinner going. It's colder than a fridge out there now, so I bet those fish are still good."

His heart was broken, but Ivy was right, and he couldn't fault her. That aspect of his life was a lot for a person to deal with. She had seen him nearly drown. That would be enough to make any sane person back away. "Okay. I'll close my eyes while you get dressed. If you'll toss me my clothes, I'll dress while you get dinner. I want to help, but…"

"I know. You can't help your ankle being hurt. I'll be back in a bit."

Kolby squeezed his eyes shut and waited for Ivy to exit the sleeping bag before zipping it back up. He rolled onto his back and covered his eyes with his arm. He wasn't sure what hurt worse, his ankle or his heart. Why had he let himself think, even for a second, that Ivy would want him? She was being nice, just as he thought.

A little voice whispered that she'd kissed him, but she was kind and caring. They were stranded on a mountain. Who knows what was going on when she did that. It didn't mean anything.

"Okay, I'm dressed. Here are your clothes. See you in a minute," Ivy said.

"Okay."

He waited for the sound of her feet crunching the ground to grow distant before unzipping his sleeping bag and poking his head out. Grabbing his shirt, he sat up and pulled it on. He rubbed his face with his hands and then looked heavenward. It was nearly dark, and the bigger stars were already glimmering.

"God, I've asked once, and I'm asking again. Please get me out of this mess. Just when I think I understand, something happens to confuse me even more. I know in my heart you're not punishing me, but it sure feels like it. Give Ivy someone who'll take care of her and treasure all she is and has to give. And if you see fit, could you do the same for me? I'm lonely, God. I've been lonely a long time, and now I've had a taste of something good. I'm not sure if I can handle being alone again."

The sound of footsteps propelled him to quickly get his jeans on. He was thankful Ivy thought to dry them. His ankle, though. When they got to civilization, he was going to need to take some time so it could heal. Maybe while he was healing, he could do a little soul-searching and figure out where he belonged in the world.

He could quit working for the Guardian Group, but that wouldn't change anything. Besides, what else could he do? Even if he stuck with just being on group protection details, his job would still be dangerous. Plus, it didn't matter what job he worked, he'd never be good enough for Ivy. But maybe if he was good enough in other areas, he could be fortunate enough to find love. Maybe.

IVY SAT WITH HER BACK AGAINST A TREE AT THE OLD campsite and wiped her eyes. She was still just a job? How could that be? After all they'd shared? He'd kissed her back, and it was incredible. Didn't he feel it? Maybe she'd been reading into it. To her recollection, that's not how it seemed at the time.

How had she gotten things so wrong? Was it just the situation messing with her head? It couldn't be. Not with the way she ached after he said saving her life was part of his job. Those words were like an arctic blast pointed right at her heart. Emotionally, she'd crab-walked away from him so fast that her little crab legs felt fatigued.

Now what was she going to do? How was she going to be stranded with him and go back to where they were?

Her stomach growled, and she held it. If she was hungry, she could only guess how hungry he was. Taking a deep breath, she closed her eyes, mentally preparing herself to face Kolby again. She could do it. She was Ivy Manning. What advice would she give herself?

"You crashed on a mountain with an attractive man. He's kept you safe and protected you. Of course you're going to have feelings for him, but the circumstances are not normal. You're trapped with him. It's just your instinct to survive kicking in. You want to survive, and you know he holds the key. All those feelings you have are just...your minds way of taking care of you. When you get down the mountain, everything will be back to normal."

There. That's what she needed. Rational and logical. An explanation and a way to deal with her body-guard until they were rescued.

Smiling to herself, she stood, grabbed her pack and the fish, and stalked back.

He was dressed and sitting up, examining his sprained ankle lying across his knee. For a second, all her determination withered. The man was beautiful. He had a kind heart and warm arms that she felt safe in…but he was doing his job. Now she needed to do hers. Get them fed so they could get some sleep.

"It's bad, huh?" she asked.

He didn't jump or look up. "I think I hit it on a rock while I was in the river. It'll be okay, though. If I stay off it tonight, we can keep going tomorrow."

She dropped the pack and set the fish down, stopping as she got to him. "You sure?"

"Yeah, gotta keep my promise to get you safely down this mountain. I don't wanna get shot by the National Guard." He lifted his head and smiled.

Again, her will to stay at arm's length took work. Her lips twitched up. "Okay. I'm going back for the other pack, and then I'll clean the fish."

"Nah, I can do that. You've done enough of the heavy lifting for today."

She lifted an eyebrow. "Really?"

He nodded. "Yep, I'm determined to be useful. I can

stay off my ankle and take care of the fish."

Ivy shrugged. "Okay, if you think you can, don't let me stand in the way. That's not my favorite thing to do." She got the fish and returned to Kolby, handing them to him.

"I don't think it's anyone's favorite thing to do." He chuckled.

"No, probably not." She glanced over her shoulder. "Well, I'll be back in a second."

"Okay."

An uncomfortable silence fell as they held each other's gazes. Maybe he'd come to the same conclusion she had. That they were better off having a professional relationship because once they got back to Nashville, they'd both realize it was the situation and nothing more.

"Okay," she said, breaking eye contact.

As she walked to get the rest of their things, she hugged herself. For all her talk, she couldn't stop feeling like her heart was in shreds. It would be okay, though. They'd eat, and she'd get some sleep. Tomorrow morning when she woke up, she'd be fine. She swallowed hard. The little voice in the back her of mind mocked her. Fine wasn't a word she was sure would ever apply to her again. She'd fallen for Kolby, and he wasn't a man you just got over.

CHAPTER 19

*A*ll through the night, Kolby had been restless with nightmares. One second he was freezing in his dream, and then Ivy would be in danger; some dreams had been a combination of both. The nightmares he'd expected, but stomach cramps weren't. It felt much like food poisoning, but he didn't understand that. He didn't think the fish were bad. They sure seemed fine.

He curled into a ball and held his midsection, sucking in a sharp breath as he knocked his ankle on the ground. What was going on with him? Why did it feel as though he was being punished?

He worked hard to put people before himself. To serve God and his country. He had plenty to be proud of, but he wasn't prideful. How many lawns had he mowed with no thanks whatsoever? How many times did he get that item off the top shelf for someone without being asked?

In the past, when he'd considered the story of Job in the Bible, he thought the man was a decent fellow, but after the last few days, Kolby had a newfound respect for him. What must it have taken to keep his faith while he lost everything and suffered?

Kolby had endured nothing close to the troubles that had befallen Job, and he'd questioned God. Now, he was questioning Him even more. Was it wrong to be weary and want relief? That's how he felt. Worn out and weary and heartsick.

Another cramp hit hard, and he grunted. He could feel the nausea building, and he knew he'd need to get some space between him and the sleeping bag soon. Only, he could barely breathe, let alone move.

The one thing he was thankful for was that Ivy had eaten a protein bar. She'd said she didn't feel like eating fish. After a bit of arguing, of course, he'd eaten his fill. He wished he'd been less of a glutton. Maybe that was what he was being taught.

"Kolby, is everything okay?" Ivy asked.

"No," he ground out. "My stomach hurts."

His sleeping bag zipped open and cool air hit his face as Ivy leaned over him. "What happened?"

"I think I have food poisoning."

"Oh, Kolby, I'm so sorry."

"Not your fault. They seemed fine to..." he said, and his sentence was cut short as a cramp hit.

She laid her hand across his forehead. "I think you have a fever too."

He nodded. That wasn't a surprise. The urge to throw up hit, and he kicked out of his sleeping bag, scrambling to a nearby tree and emptying his stomach. He wrapped one arm around the trunk to help keep himself upright, and with the other, he held his midsection. He felt Ivy's presence, and it made him drag his gaze up. He didn't want her to feel burdened to take care of him. He'd felt worse than this before.

"I'll—" Again he threw up.

"I've got water when you want it," she said and sat beside him.

"Thanks." He pulled his arm from around the tree and better positioned himself by leaning his shoulder against it. It took forever before he felt like he'd finished throwing up. He took the canteen from Ivy, rinsed his mouth out, and then took a sip. "I need to sit here a second."

"Sure. I'm right here if you need anything."

He was in a world of misery, even after throwing up. His stomach still hurt, only now it was a different kind of hurt. His muscles were sore, his head hurt, and it seemed he was bound and determined to keep his ankle in a constant state of pain.

"Ivy, saving your life was part of my job, but—"

Her hand came to rest on his shoulder. "I know, and it's okay."

"No." Kolby sucked in a sharp breath and doubled over, bracing his hand on the ground. "Saving your life was never just a job. It was always more." He wanted to say more, but he was so tired. Fog settled over his mind, and he closed his eyes.

Whatever he was about to tell her drifted away as his stomach cramps started again. He cried out as he curled into a ball. The last coherent thought he had was a prayer that God would let them be found. His strength was gone, and so was his ability to protect Ivy.

IVY SAT FACING KOLBY AS HE SLEPT. HE'D SAID protecting her was always more than a job, and she'd been thoroughly confused. Why had he said it was his job to keep her safe if he thought of her as more than that? She hated that he was sick, and selfishly, she hoped whatever he had didn't stick around too long because she had a ton of questions.

When he'd finished throwing up, she'd helped him back to the sleeping bag, and he'd collapsed on top of it. She'd set his foot on one of the packs and covered him with her sleeping bag. He'd been asleep since, and that had been hours based on how far the sun had moved. Even if he woke up that second, they'd be staying where they were.

Kolby stirred, and his eyes opened. "Are you okay?"

"I'm fine. Are you okay?"

As he sat up, he rubbed his eyes. "Yeah, I'm all right. We should get moving."

He'd thrown up over and over to the point that he'd dry heaved. The cramps he'd suffered must have been horrible for him to cry out. Up to this point, he'd handled everything with a level of pain tolerance she'd never witnessed before.

She took his hand in hers. "I know we need to get down this mountain, but you need to rest. Your ankle is hurt, and you can't tell me you aren't worn out from being sick last night."

He shook his head. "I'll rest when I know you're safely off this mountain."

What was she going to do with him? "No."

His gaze met hers. "What?"

"We're not moving. Not yet. You're hurt, tired, and sick, and you need to slow down. I doubt we would even get that far."

Pulling his gaze away, he hung his head. "Yeah, you're probably right," he said, his voice soft.

"Kolby, it's okay. It's—"

He held up his hand. "I don't want to talk right now."

"But—"

He met her gaze again. "Please, don't make me talk right now." The words were laced with such sorrow that she nearly cried.

"Okay, you get some rest."

"Thank you." He worked until he had himself inside the sleeping bag and zipped it up.

It seemed as though something had broken inside of him, and she couldn't understand why. He'd been amazing. Nothing that happened had been his fault, but it felt as if he was taking all of it on himself and holding himself to blame.

CHAPTER 20

*T*he ache in Kolby's heart extended so deep that it would take needle-nose pliers to dig it out, if it could be dug out in the first place. He'd let God down, Ivy, himself, even Noah. He could even hear the disappointment in her voice. She knew he'd failed.

It felt like he was back in his stepdad's house. He'd come home from school, and no matter how hard he tried, he was never good enough. Kolby was stupid, useless, and good for nothing. The only thing not accentuating each word was the typical smack of a belt across his backside. He could hear the crack, though. Feel the stings. For so long, he'd worked hard to make those words go away. But being on the mountain, knowing all of this was his fault...those words felt carved into his soul.

He buried his head under his arm, trying to hold back the tide of emotions filling him. Why was he so grieved all of a sudden?

The years spent in his stepdad's home were thick chains he thought he'd broken free of. He'd forgiven his mom and stepdad. Wasn't that supposed to be the end of it? He'd gone so far as to speak it daily until he felt the weight gone, but it was times like these when he wondered if it had just been giving lip service.

"I don't know what's going on, but I hope you'll listen," Ivy said as her hand came to rest on his shoulder. The pressure was lighter than usual because she was touching him through the sleeping bag.

Kolby swallowed hard, working his jaw before saying, "I'm fine."

"Well, we both know that's not true."

Had he really been that loud? Geez, he couldn't even wallow correctly. This time, he didn't respond because he wasn't sure he could keep his voice even.

"Whatever is going through that head of yours is wrong. You're a good man. Kind, patient, sweet, and thoughtful. You rented that plane for me so I could visit my family. Yeah, we crashed, but I know you well enough to know that you checked that plane from top to bottom, so it wasn't you. I also know you well enough to know you are a great pilot. You would've never offered to fly me if you didn't think you were."

He covered his mouth with his hand. How did she know to say those things? Was he that transparent?

She continued. "You've done nothing wrong, and whatever your family life was like back then has no bearing on the incredible man you are now. Your stepdad was wrong. What he did was evil, and no child should have ever been subjected to that. If anything, the man you are today is a testament to God's grace. Forgiving that man? That shows a strength of character I'm not sure I've ever seen before. Then your mom? Wow."

He slowly unzipped the bag and sat up. There was no way he could meet her eyes, not if he wanted to keep any of his dignity. He didn't know what to say, either. Thank you? How lame was that? Pathetic. That was the word. His stepdad used that one too. He'd beat Kolby and, after, tell him he was pathetic.

Ivy took his face in her hands, her cool fingers curving around his jaw, lifting his head until he had no choice but to meet her gaze. "You are a good man. Did you hear me?"

Kolby nodded. "Yeah," he whispered. And he felt even more pathetic for making her think she had to pull him out of his funk. She might have wanted to wait to move on to let him rest and recover, but that didn't mean she wanted to be stuck on the mountain with him any longer than she had to be.

"And I didn't say that stuff to boost your ego. I believe wholeheartedly what I said. You are a good man who puts others ahead of yourself. Any woman should count herself lucky to know you, and should she be loved by you…she'll be even luckier."

Just not her. Because his job was dangerous, and she didn't need to spend her life with someone she had to worry over.

Ivy circled her arms around his neck and hugged him tightly.

Would this be the last Ivy hug he got? There might be one more once they were found. He wrapped his arms around her, savoring the feel of her. If this was his last chance to have her close, he didn't want to waste it because he was feeling sorry for himself.

He buried his face in her neck, breathing in her scent and memorizing the smell. The softness of her skin, the way her touch made him feel…he wanted to memorize all of it.

"Are we interrupting something?" Noah's voice broke through the moment.

Kolby squeezed his eyes shut. He'd never live this

down. He pulled away from Ivy and found Noah standing a few feet away with a Cheshire grin on his face. Mason flanked him with a similar smile.

"It's about time you found us," Kolby said.

At least they'd been found. Now they could go home, and as soon as he mustered the courage, he'd be asking Ivy to let him out of his promise. She needed someone else to protect her.

"Gunner gave us a location as quickly as he could. We've been tracking you for just a few hours," Noah said as he crossed the distance and extended his hand to Ivy. "Miss Manning. Are you okay?"

Ivy nodded. "Well, I'm spectacular now that we've been found." She smiled.

"You've got a lot of worried people waiting on you back in Seattle."

"Seattle?" Ivy asked.

"Your parents and your manager have been on pins and needles, waiting to hear news that you're okay."

"I guess I'd feel the same way."

Mason squatted next to Kolby. "Guess it's a good thing I came, huh?"

"I guess. It's just a sprained ankle. You should check her out first. Make sure she's okay."

Ivy scoffed. "Don't listen to him. On top of spraining his ankle, his back is scraped up from sliding down a mountain, he nearly drowned, and he had food poisoning last night."

Kolby's shoulders rounded. He didn't say anything, though. All those nice words had gone in one ear and out the other once she had his failures rattled off. No, none of it was on purpose, but it didn't change the fact that he was the common denominator and the root of all the problems they'd encountered.

"Mason, please check on her first," Kolby said just above a whisper.

His friend held his gaze a moment and then stood. "Let me check you out, and I'll get to him in a minute."

Ivy grumbled but didn't say anything.

Kolby started to push off the ground, and Noah put his hand on his shoulder, staying him. "That ankle looks bad."

"Aw, it's just a sprain. I'll stay off it a few days, and it'll be fine."

"Can you put any weight on it at all?"

Why did he have to ask that? Kolby shook his head. "No, not really, but I don't think it's broken."

"Humor me, okay?"

"All right."

Noah chuckled. "No fight from you? No 'I'm fine'?"

Kolby hung his head. "I don't got no fight left in me, Noah. I just want to go home."

His friend sobered and put his hand on Kolby's shoulder. "Hey, I was kidding."

"I wasn't. I'm weary, and I don't want to talk or fight or think no more." He lifted his head a fraction. "Can we get out of here?"

"Yeah, man, we can go," Noah said and helped Kolby stand.

As soon as Kolby got to civilization, he was done with this assignment. Yes, he'd promised Ivy he'd protect her, but he wasn't physically fit to do that anymore, and keeping him on would put her in danger. She'd see he was right.

Aside from being unfit for duty, he was heartsick and in no shape to protect anyone. He needed to go home for a while, spend some time thinking, and figure a few things out before he was of any use to anyone.

CHAPTER 21

*G*lancing at Kolby for what felt like the umpteenth time, Ivy could feel the cloud surrounding him. He wouldn't look at her and barely spoke to her, and she had no idea how to help him. Truth be told, he wasn't really making eye contact or speaking to anyone. Mostly, his gaze was pinned on the flashing scenery as they were flown back to Seattle.

She had no idea what Noah and Kolby talked about while Mason was checking her out. As hard as she tried to listen in, they were talking too low for her to hear. All she knew was that Kolby wasn't acting like himself.

Noah leaned over. "Your family is waiting for you at the airport."

Oh, she'd missed her mom and dad and siblings. It wouldn't be as great as seeing them in Gatlinburg, but she'd take it. "I'll be so glad to see them. Will my manager be there as well?" Ivy hoped she would be. They'd been so angry with each other, but Ivy loved her too much to just write their friendship completely off. It was pathetic, but Ivy hoped Missy would apologize and go back to being the sweet person Ivy knew before her fame happened. She really didn't want to fire her, but she would if she needed to.

He nodded. "Yeah, she's there too."

Ivy was on cloud nine. She'd get to see her family. She and Missy could make up. And then there was Kolby. Maybe they could figure out what they were now that they were back in reality. Part of her worried, though. What if reality changed their relationship?

The thought about broke her. She loved him.

She put her hand to her mouth as the word floated in her mind.

Love. The feeling settled around her with a peace she'd never felt before. She loved Kolby Rutherford. Whether she was worthy of him was debatable, but she'd love him for as long as God let her have him. And when it was said and done, if something did happen to him before she was ready to let him go, she'd be grateful for the time she had with him.

The helicopter touching down jarred her from her thoughts. All she needed was a moment alone so she could tell Kolby how she felt. Maybe she could convince him that they could make it work. Her stalker wouldn't be around forever, and if they needed to wait, she'd wait.

Her family stood just off the tarmac, looking anxious. She suspected if one of her kids crashed on the side of the mountain, finding them alive would make her excited too.

Along with her family, an ambulance waited as well. Kolby's ankle was a lot worse than he was letting on, and Noah sensed it too. For Kolby's sake, Ivy hoped she was wrong.

Noah hopped out and held his hand out to her.

"What about Kolby?" she asked as she glanced at him again. He'd not even lifted his head. Whatever funk had fallen over him had him in its clutches, and it wasn't letting go. What had happened?

"We'll take care of him," Noah said.

"But…"

Kolby turned his head in Ivy's direction, his gaze not meeting hers. "Miss Ivy, I'm no good to you right now. As soon as my ankle is healed, I'll be back on the job. For now, you need to go spend time with your family. Noah will make sure you have protection until the stalker is found."

Miss Ivy? "What?"

"Noah, she needs to see her family," Kolby said.

Noah tugged on her arm. "Miss Manning, I'll make sure you get to see him before you fly back to Nashville, okay?"

A stun gun couldn't have hit her harder. Kolby was shut down, and she didn't understand why. What had happened in the moment between him hugging her and them being found? Maybe he was in shock or something.

"Okay, but I'm going to see him before I leave. You got it?"

Noah smiled. "Yes, ma'am. If I have to strap him down, you'll see him before you leave."

With one last look thrown in Kolby's direction, Ivy let Noah take her to her family and Missy. The hugs flew fast and furious.

When she got to Missy, her eyes and nose were red, and tears were streaming down her cheeks. "I'm so sorry, Ivy," Missy said as she threw her arms around her. "You're my best friend, and I'm so, so sorry I didn't listen. I've canceled everything, and I told the network you aren't interested in doing the show. You don't have to do anything but rest and relax."

Missy had canceled everything? "You canceled all of it?"

She leaned back. "You have nothing on your schedule for the foreseeable future. You don't even have to do the radio show. I talked to Newt, and we're both backing off." Missy pulled her into another hug. "I deserve to be fired for the way I treated you and Kolby. You were exhausted, and he was doing his job. I was the one who was out of control and ungrateful."

It was almost more than Ivy could handle. Missy had not only canceled all of her obligations, but she was sorry for the way she'd treated Kolby?

Ivy melted into her friend. She didn't know who was crying harder.

"I promise I won't be like that anymore," Missy said.

Ivy squeezed her friend tighter. "Thank you, Missy. I love you, and I know it's been hard trying to juggle all this. Maybe we'll both take a vacation, go somewhere tropical and regroup."

Missy leaned back. "Beaches and fruity drinks with umbrellas?"

Chuckling, Ivy nodded. "As many as we can guzzle."

"Is Kolby okay?"

Ivy was floored. Missy was concerned for Kolby? "He sprained his ankle, and it will need time to heal, but other than that, I think so." That was all she was willing to say about him at the moment. Until she got a second to talk to him and tell him how she felt, she was keeping anything more than that to herself.

"That's good. When I see him, I'll apologize. I'm sorry I've been such a jerk lately."

Ivy hugged her again. "I'm just glad we're okay again. I've missed my friend."

"Me too."

Ivy's dad put his arm around her shoulders. "Honey, let's take this celebration to the hotel where you can get cleaned up, and we'll get some room service, okay?"

"The first part sounds great, but after, I want to find the best burger place in Seattle and chow down," Ivy said as she covered her dad's hand with hers.

Her mom patted her cheek. "Whatever you want. We've already got a plane ready to take us back to Nashville tomorrow."

"Mr. and Mrs. Manning?" Noah stopped in front of them. "Mason will be taking Kolby's place for the time being."

Her dad nodded. "Is the young man okay?"

"He'll be fine, but with his ankle in the shape it is, he's unable to provide proper protection for Ivy."

"Well, I'm glad he's okay. Wish he wasn't hurt," her dad replied. "Is there a chance I can tell him thank you for taking care of my little girl?"

"Dad, I'm not a little girl."

"You'll always be my little girl."

Noah laughed. "He's been taken to the hospital to get his ankle checked. Once I find out more, I'll call and let you know."

Her dad shook Noah's hand. "Thank you, and I can't thank you enough for finding her."

"It was my pleasure."

"Come on, sweetheart, let's go," her mom said as she hooked Ivy's arm in hers. "Now that you've mentioned burgers, I've got a craving for one too."

Ivy caught Noah's gaze. "You have my number. Please call me when you know more about Kolby." She hoped he was listening between the lines.

He grinned. "You have my word."

Inwardly, Ivy sighed with relief. She'd spend some time with her family and Missy, and then she'd go see Kolby. Before she left Seattle, that man was going to listen to her if she had to strap him down and tape his mouth shut.

"Kolby, what's going on with you?" Noah asked as he took a seat at the foot of Kolby's hospital bed.

Why couldn't people just leave him alone? He'd arrived at the hospital, and they'd checked his ankle. It was a bad sprain. He'd torn a ligament. He'd be spending the next six to eight weeks, maybe even longer, staying off of it and letting it heal.

Kolby crossed his arms over his chest and closed his eyes, leaning his head back. He wished and prayed and hoped he could just have some peace and quiet. He was one big bruise at the moment, and he couldn't be fixed.

Noah stood and walked around the foot of the bed, facing Kolby. "Seriously, man, what's going on? I'm worried."

"Leave me alone, Noah." Kolby didn't want to talk to anyone. Nothing about his feelings or situation had changed.

"Well, tough. I don't recall you giving me a choice when I didn't want to talk. You wouldn't stop running your mouth."

Kolby worked his jaw. He and Noah were better than good friends. They were more like brothers, but right that second, Noah needed to go. "I don't want to talk, Noah. This is different, and you know it."

"You've fallen in love with Ivy Manning, and you're heartsick because you don't think she can love you."

Lifting his head, Kolby opened his eyes. "Aw, don't start."

His friend sat on the edge of his bed. "Talk to me, Kolby. I know something is wrong. This isn't like you. You've got this…fog covering you, and I don't like it."

What could Kolby say? That he was having a crisis of faith?

Noah tapped his arm. "Come on, tell me. You were the only one who didn't let me get away with my behavior when I was drinking. You set me straight. I know you don't drink, so what is it?"

The frustration began to build in Kolby. Why couldn't Noah just drop it? All Kolby needed was some time to get his thoughts in order and work through everything. He didn't need to talk about stuff.

"Kolby."

"Noah, don't."

"I'm not leaving until I know what's going on."

Kolby felt like a toddler having a tantrum in the grocery store. His ability to cope was gone.

"I feel like I'm being punished for something, and I don't know what." Kolby rattled off the sentence so fast and hard that even he was surprised by the venom in the words.

Noah tilted his head. "What on earth for?"

"I don't know. I get stuck guarding the most beautiful woman on earth, the perfect height and everything. Then I'm stupid enough to try to fly her home to Tennessee. Crash her into the side of a mountain, twist my ankle, nearly drown, and get food poisoning. I can't win for losing lately. And listen to me? Ivy is a radio person. She speaks for a living. What would she want with a defect like me? A man she can barely understand."

"First, Mia is the most beautiful woman on earth. Let's just get that straight right now."

"Shut up, Noah." Kolby rolled his eyes. He wasn't in the mood for jokes or fun.

"Yeah, you crashed, but you didn't plan that. And all those other things? You're lucky worse didn't happen. You should have been dead by the looks of that plane. Someone was looking out for you."

Logically, Kolby knew that. He knew God loved him, wanted all good things for him, and took care of him even when he didn't deserve it. At the moment, though, it wasn't his brain that was in charge. It was his heart and feelings. And he was feeling mighty low and unloved.

Kolby took a deep breath. "I'm tired. Tired of everything. I think I'm done. I'll stay on with the group, but I'll take care of the property. That's if you'll let me keep staying in that cabin."

Noah's jaw dropped. "Are you quitting?"

"Yeah. I quit. I'll write up something formal when I get a chance, but I'm finished. I want to be alone. You can't get hurt when there's no one around to do the hurting."

"But you told Ivy you'd be back on the job later."

"I know, but she would've argued if I hadn't, and she needed to see her family."

Noah exhaled heavily. "She's not going to like that. I think she has feelings for you."

"Nah, I'm just her bodyguard. Now that we're back in the real world, she'll figure that out real quick."

"I'm not so sure about that."

Kolby furrowed his eyebrows. "Why?"

"She made it clear she wanted to see you before she left for Tennessee. I called her right before I walked in the room."

There was no way Kolby could handle that, but if he said anything to Noah, his friend would hold him down if necessary. Of course, it'd be for Kolby's own good, but he just couldn't do it right that second. "All right."

Noah narrowed his eyes. "That was way too easy."

"Who's taking over for me?"

"Mason."

Kolby nodded. "Have you already told her?"

"Yeah, Mason's with her and her family now. They were letting her get cleaned up and then going to dinner."

That wasn't surprising, and he was glad she was spending time with her family. He knew how badly she'd missed them. And now he needed to ditch Noah before Ivy got to the hospital. There was no way Kolby could handle seeing Ivy again. "Okay. Hey, you think you could get me something to eat? That way, I'm not having to eat while she's here."

With a smile, Noah stood. "Yeah, I can do that. The regular?"

Kolby nodded. "Thanks." As soon as his friend was gone, Kolby was getting dressed, checking himself out, and disappearing. He'd hobble back to North Carolina and hide.

He knew Ivy would be upset with him, but it was better this way. She didn't have to try to let him down easy, and the break could be clean and...well, not pain-less, but...he didn't know. He just knew he was done. Done with all of it.

CHAPTER 22

The restaurant Ivy and her family chose was a little hole-in-the-wall, but it had been the perfect place for her family to reunite. The food was fantastic, but then again, anything would have been better than a protein bar.

Mason stood in the nearby corner like a statue, his hands clasped in front of him. It was so strange not having Kolby around. There was a different energy about Mason. Not a bad one, just...not the peace she felt when she was with Kolby. Plus, she didn't love Mason. He was a nice man, a good-looking man with his close-cut red hair, barely there five o'clock shadow, and bright-green eyes. There was a woman out there dreaming about Mason. It just wasn't her.

Ivy sat back in her chair, holding her now-stuffed

tummy. That cheeseburger had hit the spot and then some. It had been juicy, cheesy, and the best thing she'd tasted in forever. "Oh, if I eat another bite, I'll pop."

Missy bumped her with her shoulder. "Me too. This was beyond good."

Ivy's mom pulled Ivy into another hug. "I'm just glad you were found."

Ivy patted her hand. "I know, Mom."

A ring came from Ivy's jeans' pocket, and she pulled out her now-charged phone. "Oh, it's Noah." She smiled as she looked at Mason. "Hey," she said as she answered the phone.

"Kolby's in his room, and you're free to visit anytime you want," Noah said.

Ivy's heart did a backflip. "Thank you."

She spoke to Noah a few moments and then slipped her phone back into her pocket.

"What did Mr. Wolf say?" her mom asked.

"He said we could stop by anytime now and see Kolby."

"Was Mr. Rutherford okay?" her dad asked. "I'd like to shake his hand and tell him thank you for keeping you safe."

"Yeah, he's going to be okay. They're keeping him just for the night because he was dehydrated."

Her mom released her and smiled. "Good."

"I'm glad Kolby's okay," Missy said.

Wow, it was the night for surprises. "You don't hate him anymore?"

Missy rolled her eyes. "I never hated him. He just made things inconvenient when it came to your schedule. But I'll apologize to him, sincerely this time, when I see him again. I'm sorry I was such a jerk."

"Good thing my schedule has opened up. That way, Mason isn't subjected to your ire." Ivy chuckled. "I'm surprised the publisher went along with that."

"It was a tough sell, and they hoped I'd be able to talk you into finishing out the signing tour, but I stood my ground. I told them you couldn't." Missy smiled.

Ivy nodded. "You know what? That tour is only six weeks. I'll keep my commitment to them, and then I'll take my vacation. That seems like the right thing to do."

Missy's jaw dropped. "Really?" She shook her head. "No, really, it's okay. I've already told them you can't."

This was what Ivy wanted. Her friend to be in her corner and standing up for her, giving her breathing room. "No, it's okay. I'll do it."

"Are you sure? I know you've wanted a break."

"I'm sure. Thank you for listening. I needed to know you're in my corner."

Missy pulled her into a hug. "I'm always in your corner."

Ivy sighed. Yes, this was exactly what she needed. Time with her parents, her friend firmly backing her, and no pressure to be everything to everyone twenty-four hours a day. Maybe she could even write another book. Later. After she'd finished the tour and taken her needed vacation.

For now, she was going to go see Kolby. She was going to find out what was wrong and why he'd pulled away. Then she was going to kiss him and tell him she loved him and talk about aisles, flowers, houses, white picket fences, and kids.

ON THE RIDE TO THE HOSPITAL, IVY HAD MAINTAINED her courage, and then the second her big toe hit the sliding doors, it had drained out of her. She wanted to talk to Kolby. She just didn't want to hear what he had to say back.

Stuffing her hands in her coat pockets, she rocked back and forth on the balls of her feet as she waited for the elevator with her mom, her dad, and Missy...and Mason.

"Hey, Mr. Wolf," her dad said. "Getting a bite to eat?"

Ivy turned and found Noah holding a bag and a large drink.

Noah tipped his head toward Mason in greeting and shook her dad's hand as he smiled. "Well, I was hoping to get it to Kolby before you guys got here, but apparently, you were a little quicker than I was planning."

"Oh, has he not eaten yet?" Ivy asked.

Noah laughed. "Well, they brought him something...baked fish. Needless to say, he wasn't in the mood."

Chuckling, Ivy nodded. "I bet he wasn't. How is he?"

His gaze flicked from her to her mom and dad and Missy and back to her. "Uh, I'm sure he'll be glad to know there are people here to see him."

Oh, Ivy wished she'd come alone. There was something written in between the lines, and she had no idea what it was. "He seemed a little down when I last saw him."

Noah nodded. "I think he was just tired. I bet he'll be glad to see you."

The doors to the elevator opened, and they all stepped inside. Her parents chatted with Noah as they rode to the third floor. When the doors opened, they continued to chat until they reached Kolby's room.

Noah knocked on the door with his knuckles, trying to keep Kolby's drink from sloshing out. "Hey, I'm back, and you've got visitors."

When no answer came, Noah opened the door, and the room was empty.

"Where is he?" Ivy asked.

"I have no idea," Noah replied. "Maybe he just went for a walk or something. Not that he should be, but he can be pigheaded."

Noah set the food and drink on the little hospital table and stepped into the hallway. As a nurse passed by, he stopped her and asked, "Do you know where Kolby Rutherford is?"

Her eyebrows knitted together. "Uh, he checked himself out."

Swearing under his breath, Noah set his hands on his hips. "I knew he wasn't himself."

Ivy's chest tightened. "So, he just left? Did he know I was coming?"

"Yeah, I told him." Noah's hands dropped to his sides.

Kolby knew she was coming to see him, and he left anyway. Why had he done that...unless...he really thought of her as just a client and he'd been saving her feelings. But it couldn't be.

Ivy was a time-lapse photo. She went from full of life and healthy to brittle and broken in seconds.

Tears pricked her eyes. "I'd like to go to the hotel now," she whispered.

Noah cupped her elbow. "I don't know what's going on with Kolby. This isn't like him at all. Whatever it is he's dealing with, it's not you. Give him a little time, okay?"

Ivy nodded. "Sure." The word tumbled out as pieces of her cracked off and dropped to the floor. If she were a mirror, everyone in the hospital would have seven years bad luck.

Her dad put his arm around her. "Honey, let's get back to Gatlinburg and get you a little downtime, and maybe by the time you've had a little rest, he'll be ready to talk to you."

She wanted that to be true, but in her heart, she knew their talks were over. Kolby was gone, and she was alone.

CHAPTER 23

It had been two weeks since Kolby returned to North Carolina. It had taken more effort than he'd expected, but he'd managed to beat Noah back. Since his return, he'd mostly hobbled around his little cabin, or, well, shack. Between jobs, he'd been working on the place. Still, the outside looked as rough as the occupant on the inside felt.

In explicit details, Noah described how hurt Ivy had looked when they found him missing. How Noah saw her tear up. It hadn't changed Kolby's mind at all. For her sake, he needed to stay away. By now, she'd probably moved on anyway. He just hoped she was getting the time off she'd been so desperate for. Mason was now guarding her, and with him being a medic, he was probably making her rest.

As he watched the sunset, he tipped his wooden chair back, letting the back rest against the side of the house. This was what he'd needed. Silence, solitude, and peace to think. Except all his thinking had only managed to make him hurt worse.

Letting Ivy go was harder than he imagined. He stood by his decision, though. Leaving was the right thing to do, and if he had to go back...he'd have parked his rear end in that bed and told her he loved her. What he'd done was cowardly, and as much as he tried to lie to himself, it wasn't working anymore. He ached for her in a way he'd never ached for anyone.

He eased the chair down onto four legs and took a shaky breath. "I don't know what I'm supposed to do here. I hurt worse than I did before. I hurt so bad it's a bitter taste in my mouth." His nightly prayers seemed to be stuck at the light switch lately. There was no way they were hitting the heavens, or if they were, God was answering them with stony silence.

Kolby shook his head and looked upward. "Seems your lips are glued shut lately, ya know?"

Grumbling, he stood and wobbled before he braced his hand on the side of the house. "Cat got your tongue? 'Cause that still small voice is a little too still for my taste right now."

"You always talk to yourself?" Elijah asked as he stepped around the side of the house.

Kolby was in no mood to talk. He was angry, and he didn't want to say anything he'd regret. "Go away. If and when I want company, I'll let you know."

"What are you going to do? Chase me off?"

"You're a real funny guy. Now go away."

Elijah shook his head. "No. I've come to talk to you, and you're going to let me speak my piece."

"Just 'cause you talk don't mean I got to listen."

"True, but I've known you long enough to know that you'll listen even if you don't want to."

Kolby pinched his lips together. "I hate all of you. I want to be left alone. What's so difficult about that to understand?"

"Oh, I understand. I just don't buy it. Who are you mad at?"

"None of your business."

Elijah stepped onto the porch and leaned against one of the two columns holding up the porch roof. His black hair stood out against the painted sky. "It is my business. You're my friend, Kolby."

"I don't want a friend right now. I want to be…" Kolby hung his head. Oh, his heart ached. "Please, just go."

"Who are you mad at?"

"Me. Now, will you go?" In his heart, Kolby knew the answer to that wasn't himself. Kolby was mad at God. No, he was furious, and he was pretty sure Elijah knew that. All of his buddies were religious to a certain extent; they just didn't practice it as Kolby and Elijah did, and the two of them didn't push on the rest of the guys, either.

Elijah shook his head. "I've seen you mad at yourself, but this goes beyond that. I'm going to keep asking until you give me the real answer."

Kolby growled in frustration. "Fine. I'm mad at God. You happy?"

"No, and I don't understand why."

"Why?" His voice rose an octave. "I'm sick and tired of being hurt all the time."

Straightening, Elijah shrugged. "Whose fault is that? It's not God's."

"He's the one in control, ain't He?"

"Yeah, but the reason you're hurting right now has nothing to do with God and everything to do with you. You're so focused on the hurting that you missed the good stuff."

"I don't know what you're talking about. There's no good stuff."

Elijah grunted. "Liar. You're miserable because you're choosing to be."

Choosing to be miserable? Kolby wasn't doing that. "I am not."

"You skipped out on Ivy. I'd say that was a choice."

Kolby jerked his gaze to Elijah.

"Oh, yeah, Noah told me. He told all of us."

"She isn't going to want the likes of me."

Elijah scoffed. "You can control a lot of things, but you can't control who loves you. Go tell that woman you love her. From the sounds of it, she has feelings for you too."

Shaking his head, Kolby sat again. "I've hurt her, and there's no way she'd give me the time of day. I've missed my chance."

"No, you haven't. The only thing you're missing right now is a plane to Nashville."

Kolby lifted his gaze to Mason's. "Nashville? She was supposed to be in Gatlinburg."

"Well, from what I understand, she was in the middle of her book tour and had a huge panic attack. She's at home right now, taking a break. But from what Noah says, she'll be back on the road in a few days." Elijah stepped off the porch onto the ground. "I'd say that's your window of opportunity to go grovel. Just tell her you love her. You can't possibly be more miserable than you are right now."

Pinching the bridge of his nose, Kolby closed his

eyes as he tried to wrangle his thoughts. Elijah was right. He'd been so angry that he'd missed the best thing to come his way. If he'd stayed put in that hospital, there was no telling what would have happened. He'd been feeling so sorry for himself that he'd laid that on Ivy when she'd never treated him like a charity case.

"I'll see you later, man. Just think about what I said." Elijah turned to leave.

"Wait!"

"Yeah?"

"I need a ride to the airport."

"I'm sure Noah would let you use the jet." Elijah smiled.

Kolby grunted. "He's probably ticked at me too."

"No, I was worried," Noah said as he turned the corner.

"Were the two of you gonna gang up on me?" asked Kolby.

Elijah chuckled.

Noah shook his head. "No, I've got two pieces of information I thought you'd want."

Kolby knitted his eyebrows together. "Okay."

"First, I got a call from the FAA about your crash."

"They tell you it was my fault?"

Noah shook his head. "No, it wasn't your fault.

Lightning melted the wiring, and there was no way you could have taken that plane any farther. And from what they tell me, it took real skill to land that plane like you did and walk away."

Kolby worked his jaw as he nodded. It wasn't his fault, just a freak accident. He didn't have a choice but to strand them if they wanted to survive. "And the second?"

"We've found Ivy's stalker, or we think so. Police are still questioning her. It was a woman who was jealous of her. Ryder hasn't been able to link her to the nicotine she used to poison you, but the IP address matches the emails."

"A woman? Didn't see that coming," Kolby said.

"Yeah, lives in the same neighborhood too, so she had the chance to mess with that delivery. It all fits, but we'll see what happens with the interrogation." Noah caught Kolby's gaze. "Mason will need a ride back once they're sure they have the right person in custody. You could hitch a ride there to pick him up. That's if you still want to visit Nashville."

Kolby grinned. "Yeah, I'd like that, but you know this means I really do quit."

Noah nodded. "I figured as much, but it's not like I didn't do same when I married Mia. Yeah, I'm in charge, but you don't see me stepping in front of bullets. I'd like to keep you in the Guardian Group in some capacity, though."

Grunting a laugh, Kolby smiled. "How about that ride now?"

WITH HER LEGS CURLED UNDER HER, IVY STARED OUT the front window of her home.

"Here," Missy said, handing her some hot tea and taking a seat next to Ivy. "I think we should be celebrating with wine, but it's your celebration, so tea it is."

The stalker had been caught, at least in Ivy's mind. The police were questioning a woman in her neighborhood. She lived a few blocks over, and a load of emails were found on her server. Ryder and Mia were both pretty confident it was her, but until there was an arrest, Mason was staying in place. At the moment, he was in the spare bedroom.

She rubbed the spot over her heart. It had been Kolby's room, and anytime she thought of him, an ache as deep as the ocean would hit her. Ivy took the cup Missy offered. "I guess you're happy too. As soon as the police make an arrest, there won't be any bodyguards gumming up the works."

Missy shrugged. "It's been a pain, but I did want you safe."

"You didn't like Kolby." Ivy leveled her gaze at Missy. "Admit it."

"I didn't dislike him. I knew he'd break your heart, and I didn't want to see you hurt. In the process, I was the one who was doing the hurting, and I'm so sorry. I wish I could take it all back. All of it. You didn't need a manager; you needed a friend."

In the weeks following Kolby's disappearance, Ivy had confided in Missy a little, telling her about how she felt for Kolby and what they'd shared while they were stranded. Ivy had shed more than her fair share of tears over him too.

To keep her mind off of him, she'd started on the book tour almost immediately, and it had been going well until a few days ago. A panic attack had hit in the middle of her signing. She'd done all the techniques her therapist taught her. None of it had helped, and she'd passed out in the middle of a bookstore in front of everyone.

Ivy was so embarrassed that she'd flown back to Nashville so she could take a few days and regroup before returning to the same bookstore to make up for her abrupt departure.

Missy sniffed the air. "Oh, those cookies smell so good."

"Not as good as Grandma's brownies."

"I've never understood why you don't like coconut cookies. They're incredible." Missy bumped Ivy's shoulder with hers. "But thank you for making them for me."

"You're welcome. I had the ingredients anyway."

Missy nodded. "Those are Kolby's favorite too, aren't they?"

"Yeah," Ivy said just above a whisper.

She'd found out he shared Missy's love for the cookies when he first got there. She'd baked them for Missy after they'd had an argument and she was taking her a peace offering. That night, it was the first time he'd ever come back out after going to bed for the night. He'd wandered into the kitchen, she'd offered him a few cookies, and he'd gobbled them down before shuffling back to his room.

Her lips twitched up as she remembered him blushing after he realized he'd eaten half of them. It had been the first time she'd seen him do that and the first time she'd fantasized about kissing him. She'd been able to do plenty of dreaming that night while she stayed up baking a few more.

"Why aren't you furious with him?" Missy asked.

Ivy shrugged. She didn't have an answer for that. At least not one Missy would understand. When she'd first returned, she'd been beyond hurt and angry, promising herself that if she ever saw him, she'd sock him in the nose. But as she thought more about it, she knew there had to be more going on than she understood. He'd never have hurt her like that if there wasn't.

The doorbell rang, and Missy gave Ivy a funny look. "It's almost ten. Are you expecting someone?"

Mason came out of the back bedroom, gun drawn, catching Ivy's gaze.

Ivy shrugged, and Mason eased closer to the door.

"Ivy." Kolby's voice carried through the door. "I know you're probably so mad at me you could spit nails, but would you talk to me just a second?"

Ivy wanted to burst into tears. She'd been praying and praying he'd come to her when he was ready to talk. She just knew something had happened, and whatever it was, it wasn't something she could change. Another thing Missy wouldn't understand.

Spending those few days on the mountain with Kolby had rekindled her relationship with God. She spent most of her mornings reading her Bible and having little talks with Him. Ivy loved Missy, but faith wasn't something Ivy could share with her friend.

Missy rolled her eyes. "Want me to tell him to go away?"

"Uh, no, I want to do that myself. The cookies smell like they're done. You get those out and let me talk to him, okay?"

"You sure?"

Ivy nodded and stood. "I need to handle this myself if I'm going to get closure."

"Okay, but don't be too nice," Missy said as she pushed off the couch, eyeing Mason on her way to the kitchen.

"You can let him in, Mason," Ivy said. Kolby was at her home, wanting to talk, and she couldn't thank God enough.

Mason smiled and holstered his weapon, opening the door. "It's about time, you idiot."

Kolby rubbed the back of his neck. "Yeah, I know."

"I think you'll be fine if I take a long walk," Mason said. "You think you'll be okay?"

Nodding, Kolby glanced at Ivy and said, "I think so."

Crossing the room, Ivy stopped at the door and wiped her palms down her pajama bottoms. The second her gaze touched him, she felt jittery. Her heart buzzed in her chest, and her breath caught. "Hi."

Jeans, t-shirt, one boot, and balanced on crutches, he was the best thing Ivy had laid eyes on in weeks.

Mason flicked his gaze from Kolby to Ivy and mock saluted as he trotted out of the house. "See you guys in a little while."

Before she could say another word, he said, "Hey, I'm sorry I'm here so late. I just…" He dropped his gaze to the porch floor. "I owe you an apology for leaving like I did. I know I don't deserve your forgiveness or your kindness after the way I treated you, but I hope you can find it in your heart to forgive me."

She stepped aside, inviting him in with the wave of her hand. "Come inside. It's freezing out there."

He hobbled inside, and as she shut the door, he faced her. "I am so sorry."

"What happened?"

Missy peeked her head around the corner of the kitchen. "Uh, before you guys get too deep in conversation, I'm going to take a few cookies and get going." She grabbed her purse, stopped at the door, and looked from Kolby to Ivy. "If you need anything, let me know."

"Thanks, I will," Ivy said.

Missy smiled and dashed out the door, shutting it behind her.

Ivy motioned to the couch. "How about you sit down and fill me in on why you disappeared?"

Kolby moved to the couch and dropped down hard. "Thank you."

Before she sat down, she pulled the coffee table closer, set a pillow on top, and rested his foot on it. "There. Now talk."

For a moment, he sat with his gaze pinned on the coffee table, and then he took a deep breath, bringing his gaze to Ivy's. "I told you I forgave my mom and stepdad, and I absolutely believed I had. But I hadn't. I carried that man's abuse around with me everywhere I went. All those things he said about me shaped my opinion of myself. I never admitted that they did because I'd lied to myself long enough to believe it."

Ivy's heart beat faster as he spoke. He was giving her a piece of himself. A part that she'd need to guard and hold like it was precious. "Okay."

"I let them color how I thought other people saw me too."

"Like me?"

He nodded. "Yeah, like you. You speak well. You talk for a living, and here I am, some worthless, stupid hick who has nothing to offer you."

Tears pricked her eyes. "Kolby, no, that's not true."

"I know...now, but it took a little soul-searching to

come to that, and even after knowing it, it was hard to admit that I'd been wrong, and I knew I'd hurt you."

"I was hurt, but I knew you weren't yourself. I could see it in your eyes before we were rescued."

He took her hand in both of his and touched the back of it to his lips. "I have nothing to offer you except my heart, Ivy. I'll never be sophisticated or refined or any of that, but I'll love you better than anyone who is."

Ivy's lips parted with a tiny gasp.

Continuing, he said, "I love you more than anything on this earth, and if you'll give me the opportunity, I'll love you as long as you'll let me."

He loved her. He *loved* her. The most precious three words to ever tickle her ears. Ivy threw her arms around his neck and buried her face in his shoulder as tears streamed down her face.

"I'm sorry. I didn't mean to make you cry," Kolby said as his arms wrapped around her.

She chuckled. "Not all tears are sad." She leaned back and smiled. "I love you too."

"You do?" He sounded almost shocked, which baffled her. "But you kissed me and then apologized. Why?"

She chewed her lip a second. "I pulled away because it scared me. I already had strong feelings for you, and to think I could have even stronger feelings and then lose you..." She shook her head. "Your job is dangerous. The thought of falling in love with you and then losing you terrified me. It had nothing to do with your skills. At least not in the kissing department."

"I thought—"

With a sigh, she smiled. "I love you and have loved you. I was going to tell you that the night you left, but I didn't get the chance."

"Aw, it was probably for the best. I doubt I would've heard you." He traced her jaw with his fingertips. "I was hurting too bad to really hear anyone."

"I'm so sorry you were hurting. If that happens again, tell me."

"I will. I'll never do that again."

Taking his face in her hands, she touched her lips to his. "I love you, Kolby Rutherford," she said as they locked eyes. "I love you with all my heart. All those things like sophistication and refinement...they don't translate to being loved. I'd rather be loved than look like I'm being loved. You are who I want. I want you for as long as I can have you."

He smiled as he hugged her tightly. "I'd really like that to translate to forever."

"I can make that work."

Cupping her cheek, he pulled her lips to his, and she was in heaven. He loved her, he wanted to be with her, and he was talking about forever. And oh, how she loved his kisses. They were never rushed. It was like he savored her with each brush of his lips. This was the kind of love she'd been wanting. The kind that wanted her and only her.

When he deepened the kiss, a tiny moan escaped her. It was the best kiss she'd shared with him because it spoke of a long-lasting, soul-tied, becoming-one type of love. He ran his hand up her back, into her hair, and held her as the kisses turned more demanding.

How long they kissed, she had no idea. All she knew was she was struggling to breathe when he broke it. Burying his face in her neck, he inhaled deeply.

Silently, she said a prayer of thanks as she hugged him again. It had taken a couple of weeks, but God had answered her prayers and Kolby's, and for that, she wasn't able to express enough gratitude.

Kolby was hers. She was his. And it happened just as it was supposed to.

CHAPTER 24

*I*vy loved him. She'd accepted his apology, and she loved him and wanted forever. Kolby couldn't have asked for more. The amount of mercy he'd experienced wasn't lost on him either. Yeah, bad things had happened, but even better were the good things. "I missed you."

She kissed the side of his face. "I missed you too. It wasn't the same without you here. Mason is nice, but he's no Kolby Rutherford."

Laughing, he leaned back and pushed her hair over her shoulder. "I'm just glad the stalker is in custody."

"Me too. That's what Missy and I were celebrating." She chewed her lip. "Would you like some cookies?"

His eyes widened. Oh, man, he loved those cookies, and he'd smelled them as he'd crutched his way to the door. "I thought I smelled coconut cookies, but kissing you was way more important." That last part was truer than true.

With a chuckle, she kissed him. "Way more important, but I think we can take a break for some cookies and milk."

"I love those cookies, and milk would be great to wash them down."

"Would you believe those are Missy's favorite too?"

His jaw dropped. "You mean I have something in common with her? Well, more than one thing. You."

"You wouldn't believe it, but she's been so great. Patient with me. Backing me up when I don't want to do something."

"Elijah said you were on the book tour again."

She nodded. "Yeah, it was a commitment I felt I needed to keep. I was a little heartsick when I got home, and I needed a distraction."

That hit him right in the chest. "I'm sorry for my part in that."

"Once I had a second to calm down, I was okay."

"Yeah?" He tilted his head.

"I've been having coffee of a morning before my day starts, reading my Bible, and talking to God. Needless to say, you were the topic of many discussions."

Kolby lowered his gaze. "You were in mine too."

Ivy cupped his cheek, and he pressed his face into her palm. "I'm just glad you came to see me, even if it is crazy late."

"Yeah, Elijah kinda set me straight."

She grinned. "I need to thank him, then."

"He said you had a panic attack. Why?"

Shrugging, she said, "I don't know. One second I was fine, and then the next, I couldn't breathe."

"I should have been there."

"It's okay. You're here, and you're not leaving me ever again."

He shook his head. "No, I'm not. I've told Noah I'm done with the dangerous stuff. Maybe I'll be on call or something. We'll see."

"Really?"

"Yeah, I liked the work, but I love you more."

Ivy grinned. "You didn't have to do that, but I can't say that doesn't give me some peace."

Kolby kissed her. "Then it's worth it."

Her smile widened. "I'm going to go get the cookies while they're still warm."

Still-warm coconut cookies. His blessings were piling up. "Okay."

She stood, bent down, and kissed him before going

to the kitchen. As she returned, he smiled up at her. "Those really do smell amazing."

"Meh, not as good as my grandma's brownies."

"Let me get the milk. The plate was still warm, and I didn't want to drop it by trying to carry too much all at once," she said as she set them on the coffee table.

He plucked a cookie off the top and took a giant bite. "Okay, I—"

The second the morsel hit his tongue, his head started spinning, and he knew something was wrong. He dropped the cookie back on the plate. "Ivy, don't touch those." He grabbed the dishtowel she'd brought with her to carry the hot plate and spit out the bite he'd taken. He remembered this feeling from when he picked up the package.

Her eyebrows knitted together. "Are you okay?"

Nausea hit, and he shook his head. "No."

"Get away from him, Ivy," Missy said.

Ivy looked up and over to the hallway leading to the bedrooms. "Missy?" Where had she come from? Then she remembered Missy had a key. She must have come through the back door. How long had she been listening in on them?

She stepped into the light, and Ivy noticed the gun she was holding. "Get away from him."

Ivy held Missy's gaze. "What are you doing?"

"Things were going so well without him. If he'd just stayed out of the picture. You were doing the book tour, warming up to other things. He ruins everything."

Despite his head swimming, Kolby stood and faced Missy. "You poisoned the package too?" And in Kolby's heart, he knew Missy had set the other woman up.

"I just wanted you to stay in Tennessee during our trip to Seattle. Ivy was on her way to the top until you dropped into our lives. Do you know what it's taken to get those network executives to be patient enough for me to talk her into doing the show? I was getting close too. Biding my time. But no, you had to show up again. If only I'd had a little more of the nicotine left, we wouldn't even be talking. But I'll take what I can get."

Kolby swayed and tried to stop himself from falling and failed. He crumpled to the floor, his head cracking against the coffee table on the way down.

"Kolby!" Ivy screamed.

"Back away from him, Ivy," Missy barked.

His head felt like a busted melon, and he was poisoned. Missy also had a gun trained on Ivy, and he needed to keep her from getting hurt. He worked to control his breathing and keep the nausea at bay. He needed to get Mason back. Slipping his hand into his pocket, he pulled it up just enough to dial his number.

In the meantime, he'd stay still and hope Missy got close enough to disarm her. Maybe she'd make a mistake and think he was knocked out, and then he could make his move.

BLINDSIDED. THAT WAS THE BEST WORD TO DESCRIBE how Ivy was feeling. "Missy, what's going on? What are you doing?"

Missy raked her hand through her hair. "I'm taking care of a problem, just like I always do. You have a career that I've worked hard on, and I'm not letting a guy take it away from us." She motioned with the gun. "Now move away from him."

"Please don't." Ivy touched her fingers to her lips. "Please, Missy. Don't hurt him. He's a good man."

"You have too much to do to be in a relationship with anyone. You…you have to do that show. They're offering you a ton of money, an apartment in Seattle, and so many other perks. You have to do it."

"Why? Would you please tell me what's going on? Why do I have to do it?"

"Because…because I made some bad investments,

and I've got bad people coming after me. If I don't get you to take that job, I don't get my percentage, and I'm in trouble."

In trouble? That's why Missy had been pushing her so hard? "You could have just come to me. Told me what was going on. I would have helped you."

Missy scoffed. "Oh yeah, the perfect Ivy would help me with loan sharks?"

"Of course I would have. You're my best friend." Ivy stole a glance at Kolby. He was too still, and his breathing looked so shallow. He'd hit his head so hard. What if he was really hurt?

"Don't even think about it." Missy took a step forward, waving the gun at Ivy. "I don't know what you see in this guy. The stalker was in custody, and you were free of all these bodyguards."

A strange feeling settled over Ivy, and she narrowed her eyes. "You're my stalker?"

"It wasn't supposed to get so out of control. Just a little publicity to help boost your career. Then you started giving me grief about everything, and I just... it kept you close and distracted. At least it did, until this jerk showed up." Missy stepped closer to Kolby and drew her foot back like she was going to kick him.

Ivy lunged forward. "No."

The front door flew open, and Mason stood in the doorway with a gun at the ready. "Stop!"

With a snarl, Missy jerked her gun toward Mason, glancing from Mason to Kolby.

Kolby sat up, grimaced, and touched his head as he leaned his back against the couch. "About time you showed up."

Mason grunted a chuckle. "Put the gun down, Missy."

Missy's eyes narrowed. "Put your gun down, or I'll shoot him."

Ivy held her hands up. "Missy, stop. Mason is a trained professional. He's not going to miss, and you're going to get yourself killed."

For a moment, Ivy wondered if Missy would shoot Kolby just out of hate, even if it meant Mason would kill her. The tension in the room grew until the point that Ivy thought she'd choke. Slowly, Missy lowered the gun.

"Set the gun on the floor and take two steps back," Mason said.

Missy did as Mason commanded as he kept his weapon trained on her.

Ivy was crushed. This woman had been her friend, or pretended to be, for years. All this time she'd been the one sending her all those horrible emails? "You sat on my couch tonight, celebrating the capture of my stalker when it was you all along. Who was the poor woman who was arrested?"

Missy's lips curled into a snarl. "You find a lot of talent on the internet. I just paid someone to make sure the emails looked like they were coming from someone else. The only reason whoever it was got arrested was because the person I used got lazy. Once they arrested that woman, I knew I had to stop."

Ivy was struggling to process everything. She kneeled next to Kolby and touched his head. "So, all this time, you were just pretending to be my friend?"

Missy sighed. "Not at first. Not even right after the column went viral and you got the radio show. I was your friend."

"Was?"

"You didn't appreciate me. I worked to get you famous, and all you ever did was complain. Do you know what I would have given to have the attention you have? And you got it because of some dumb advice that was warm and fuzzy."

Kolby wrapped his free hand around Ivy's waist and pulled her close. "Don't listen to her. She's just being cruel 'cause she got caught. You give good advice."

Missy cursed under her breath. "I'm done talking."

"Great. Lie facedown on the floor with your hands behind your back," Mason said as he pulled out his phone, putting it to his ear. He relayed what had happened quicker than Ivy ever could. When he was finished, he ended the call and slipped the phone back into his pocket.

"Are you okay?" Ivy asked Kolby.

"I don't feel good, and my head hurts."

Keeping his gun trained on Missy, Mason made his way over to Kolby and squatted in front of him. "My bag is in my room, and normally, I'd hand you my weapon, but I'm not sure you could stop her."

"I couldn't," Kolby replied.

"And if Ivy retrieved my bag, I don't think she could hold a gun on Missy while I worked on you."

She eyed the gun and shook her head. "No."

Mason gripped Kolby's shoulder, squeezed it, and stood.

Ivy pressed her forehead to Kolby's shoulder. Missy's betrayal stung, but not as much as it should have. When had their friendship changed? Why didn't she see it sooner?

Kolby rubbed her back. "You loved her, and that covers a multitude of sins. You have a beautiful heart, and her kind of darkness doesn't make sense to you."

Ivy lifted her head and caught Kolby's gaze. "How did you know I was thinking that?"

"It's what I'd be thinking."

"Thank you." Ivy leaned her head against his shoulder again as the wail of police cars and ambulances drew their attention to the front window.

Ivy had lost her best friend, but in her heart, she knew she'd lost her long ago. It didn't ease the hurt she was experiencing one bit. But she did have Kolby who would love her through it. And that helped soften the ache.

CHAPTER 25

"I don't need to stay overnight. I've got a bump on the head, and that's all," Kolby said. How was it he kept ending up in the one place he hated the most?

Ivy combed her fingers through his hair. "It's more than a little bump. You have a concussion, and you were poisoned. They need to keep you for observation."

"It's a bump. I can see clearly. I'm not foggy. I'm fine."

"And you're staying put even if I have to strap you to the bed."

"Aw, Ivy—"

Her lips spread into a thin line, and she lifted an eyebrow. Based on the look she was giving him, he'd officially hit the end of her tolerance for nonsense. She narrowed her eyes. "You are not leaving."

"Fine," he grumbled.

"Knock-knock," Noah said as he walked into the room.

"Hey," Kolby said.

"I thought you guys might like to know that the woman we were questioning was let go a few hours ago. Ryder and Mia remotely accessed Missy's laptop. Which, Mia was both appalled and elated that she didn't have a password on it. It was Missy the whole time. She's in a ton of debt. And that nicotine? She has a half-brother in North Carolina, and he sold it to her. Authorities are on their way to pick him up for questioning as we speak."

Ivy sighed. "I can't believe it was her. We've been friends forever."

Noah shrugged. "Some people change for the better, while others change for the worse. She did a good job masking her true colors."

"See, I told you," Kolby said.

Ivy cast her gaze to the floor. "I know."

Kolby knew her heart was hurting. As poorly as Missy had treated her, Ivy couldn't just turn off loving her, and the betrayal cut Ivy to the core. "Doesn't change the hurt."

Ivy shook her head. "No, it doesn't."

Noah shook Kolby's hand and then Ivy's. "Okay, I've got to get going. I'll talk to you later." He turned and strode out of the room.

Ivy stretched out next to Kolby and rested her arm across his chest. He kissed the top of her head, wishing he knew how to soothe her ache. Hurt he knew, betrayal even, but a friend pretending was something he didn't know or understand.

"I wish I had words of wisdom for you," he said.

Lifting on her elbow, Ivy nodded. "It's okay. It hurts, but the loss is more like a hangnail than a cut. I think I was so used to her friendship that I wasn't willing to really examine it."

"I can understand. It was comfortable, and what little I got to see, you didn't have much time for anything familiar, so having her around helped."

"Yeah, exactly." She smiled. "Will you tell me how you're really feeling?"

"Really, I'm okay. They gave me some charcoal for the poison, and that fixed it. My head's a little sore and so is my ankle. That fall set me back a little."

Nodding, she brushed the back of her hand along his cheek. "My heart was in my throat when you hit your head. It was so loud, and the angle…I didn't know how badly you were hurt."

"It rang my bell for sure, and I almost passed out. But I knew I couldn't. Not with that gun trained on you."

Ivy touched her lips to his, moving them slowly against his. "I think your hero punch card got filled tonight."

Kolby snorted. "Hero punch card?"

"Uh-huh. With every deed, you get a stamp."

"What do I get now that it's full?"

She grinned and lowered her lips to his.

To Kolby, that was the perfect response. Her kisses, her love, and a future with her. There had been a lot of pain to get to this point, but being truly free was worth it. It made being loved by Ivy that much sweeter.

EPILOGUE

Thanksgiving that same year...

From the back window of Ivy's family home, she could see snow coming down in sheets. Savory, sweet, and fruity smells filled the air as she and her mom and sister bustled around in the kitchen finishing up the last few Thanksgiving dishes.

"Mrs. Manning, you need me to get more firewood?" Kolby asked, snagging a roll.

Ivy moved to pop his hand, but he pulled away too quickly. "You stop that."

"They're good, and I'm hungry. You can't fill a house with these kinds of smells and expect no one to snack."

"You'll fill up on bread and be too full to eat anything else."

Ivy's mom waved her off. "Kolby, first, I told you to call me Kathy or Mom. Second, yes, we do need more firewood, but you aren't the only one who knows how to chop wood. And third, Ivy, let him have a roll. I've seen that boy eat. I don't think he gets full."

Her mom did have a point. She'd learned that he had a hollow leg when it came to food, especially when it came to home-cooked meals. This was their first holiday together with her family, and she loved how he fit. He was the piece she'd been missing all this time.

Of course, he was still on call with the Guardian Group if they needed anything, but he'd stopped doing anything that put him in danger. Mostly because Ivy's dad had asked him to stay on as her protection when she did appearances and such. The ordeal with Missy had spooked her dad, and he loved Kolby. Her whole family did.

He wrapped his arm around Ivy's waist, planting a quick kiss on her lips. "See? She knows I can't ruin my appetite."

Ivy leaned back. "You've charmed my momma and turned her against me."

Finishing the roll, he swiped his hand down his jeans. "Aw, no I haven't."

She circled her arms around his neck. "Have too, but I'll forgive you since I love you so much."

"I love you too." Kolby held her gaze almost too long. "I was going to wait and plan something special, but I don't want to wait anymore."

Ivy tilted her head. "Wait for what?"

Her jaw dropped as he went to one knee. Her mom gasped, clapping her hands together.

"I've never loved anyone the way I love you, and I feel blessed to have met you," he said, pulling a ring box from his back pocket and opening it. "I'd consider it an honor and a privilege if you'd be my wife."

Tears pooled in Ivy's eyes. She loved Kolby more than anyone and couldn't imagine spending her life with anyone else. "I'd love to be your wife."

He slipped the ring on her finger, stood, and lifted her by the waist as he kissed her. "I love you. I always will."

Their lips met again, and it had to be the best, sweetest, most glorious kiss she'd ever had. Kolby had been hers for months, and now he'd officially be hers forever. She'd be Mrs. Kolby Rutherford, and she couldn't think of a better future.

Ivy smiled. "I love all of you, and I always will."

A Clean Fake Relationship Romance Book One

The Star's Fake Marriage:
A Clean Fake Relationship Romance Book Two

The Bodyguard's Fake Marriage:
A Clean Fake Relationship Romance Book Three

The Matchmaker's Fake Marriage:
A Clean Fake Relationship Romance Book Four

The Beast's Fake Marriage:
A Clean Fake Relationship Romance Book Five

A Clean Army Ranger Romance Series:

The Ranger's Chance:
A Clean Army Ranger Romance Book One

The Ranger's Heart:
A Clean Army Ranger Romance Book Three

The Ranger's Hope:
A Clean Army Ranger Romance Book Four

Clean Romance Stand Alones:

Love and Charity

The Mistletoe Game:

A Clean Christmas Novella

ABOUT THE AUTHOR

Bree Livingston lives in the West Texas Panhandle with her husband, children, and cats. She'd have a dog, but they took a vote and the cats won. Not in numbers, but attitude. They wouldn't even debate. They just leveled their little beady eyes at her and that was all it took for her to nix getting a dog. Her hobbies include...nothing because she writes all the time.

She loves carbs, but the love ends there. No, that's not true. The love usually winds up on her hips which is why she loves writing romance. The love in the pages of her books are sweet and clean, and they definitely don't add pounds when you step on the scale. Unless of course, you're actually holding a Kindle while you're weighing. Put the Kindle down and try again. Also, the cookie because that could be the problem too. She knows from experience.

Join her mailing list to be the first to find out

publishing news, contests, and more by going to her website at https://www.breelivingston.com.

facebook.com/BreeLivingstonWrites

twitter.com/BreeLivWrites

bookbub.com/authors/bree-livingston

Made in the USA
Monee, IL
11 November 2019